THE LEOPARD WHO
CLAIMED A WOLF

SARAH MAKELA

THE LEOPARD WHO CLAIMED A WOLF

BOOK SIX

When a wolf loves a leopard...

He's her protector...

Caitlyn Fraser, a wereleopard who has always hated cruel werewolves, is the former prisoner turned mate of Dougal Sterling, Alpha of the Scottish pack. She's courting jeopardy with her determination to attend the funeral of her brother's father, since the Pack blames her for Alistair's death. But still Dougal protects her from his wolves.

Her defender...

Short of allies, Dougal struggles to balance loyalty and attention between the Pack and Caitlyn. When the Pack's stability crumbles, he's faced with the return of his older brother, the rightful Alpha, who shirked his duty after their father's death. However, Ewan's challenge will be a battle to the death. Sheltering Caitlyn can only lose Dougal more friends, but he knows she's the mate he's longed for.

But survival takes two...

Menace lurks in every corner of the Highlands; Alistair and Ewan's supporters and haters of shapeshifters abound. Caitlyn and Dougal must stick together, pushing back fiercely when they are attacked. Even if that puts them in mortal danger…

Sign up for Sarah's newsletter for her latest news, giveaways, excerpts, and much more!
http://bit.ly/SarahMakelaNewsletter

Editor: Word Vagabond

Cover Artist: The Killion Group

ISBN-10: 1-942873-89-1

ISBN-13: 978-1-942873-89-1

CAITLYN

*T*he driveway leading up to the Scottish Pack's massive headquarters stretched almost half a mile. I rested my chin on my arms and stared out of the Alpha's window on the second story, overlooking the circular section of the drive. The Pack's castle came complete with its very own dungeon, but at least they weren't keeping me in there anymore. The memory of Alistair's craggy face haunted my dreams each time I closed my eyes. His brutal fists hammered away against my face, ribs, and stomach, until I could no longer sleep.

Tension radiated through my shoulders, and I balled my hands into fists. No, Alistair—Colin's father—was dead. Dougal had protected me, and my brother, from that monster when I didn't have the strength to fight back.

Not that it mattered.

Two days had passed since my brother's sudden departure. Now Colin was on his own with no one to watch his back. How could he leave without saying anything to me? I flexed my fists again, welcoming the anger as it bubbled up in my chest and replaced my sadness.

The heavy weight of a man's hand descended on my back. I twisted around, my knuckles connecting with a solid jaw lined with dark, coarse stubble. A familiar jaw. *Shite.*

Dougal stumbled back half a step, but then he planted his feet like a tree with strong roots, not budging any further. Sharp power flared outward from him before he squelched it, stretching the muscles in his jaw. A frown tugged at his lips, and the corners of his eyes creased, either in pain or displeasure.

"Dougal! I'm so sorry." The sudden movement of punching him had shot a searing ache through my battered ribs again. The pain stole my breath away, but I tried to force it down. How could I have been so careless? If he'd been anyone else in the Pack, I would've caused World War III.

"Dinnae fash. The punch bloody well hurt, though. I didn't realize you were so strong." Dougal's frown melted away as he pulled me closer and pressed a kiss to my forehead. "Seems like you're recovering your strength." His gaze drifted past me to the long gravel driveway of the estate. "How are you doing, love?"

The emotions I'd been stomping down now bubbled to the surface again. "I cannae believe Colin left me. He left before I even regained consciousness. How could he?" With anyone else, I wouldn't show weakness, but I rested my forehead against Dougal's chest, needing his touch and savoring his warmth. "I barely had time to talk with him, and when I did, it wasn't a good time to ask how he was doing after the months he'd spent in that bloody research facility—or even to ask where he would go to heal…"

Tears welled in my eyes, but I held them back, refusing to cry. "I gave up so much—my job, my flat, my life—while trying to track him and bring him home. What if my sacrifices were all for naught?"

"Nae, they weren't for naught, love." Dougal kissed the

top of my head. "I know you're hurting. You have plenty of reasons to be, but the man who came back wasn't the same one who left for the United States." He lifted my chin, forcing me to see the sincerity in his clear blue eyes. "Whatever those scientists did affected him in ways neither of us will probably ever know. Waiting at the window won't make him return any sooner." He wrapped his arms around me and gently pulled me against his chest again. "Let me draw you a bath. Remember, I'm here if you need to talk."

He was right, even if I didn't want to admit it. Waiting for Colin's return wouldn't help, but what else could I do? "I know, but that doesn't make this any easier for me. He's my younger brother. I feel helpless that I cannae be there for him...again." A heavy ache settled on my heart, and I pulled away hating the awkward emotions crushing me. "Sorry."

Dougal turned away from me and stared out of the window again. His jaw clenched and unclenched, as if he were trying hard to hold in his words. A lot was going on in his life too, and yet he was making a strong effort to support me through my problems. Things had become increasingly strained between him and his Pack since my arrival and Duncan and Alistair's subsequent deaths. He didn't talk about what he faced, and I didn't want to pressure him.

After a few moments of silence, he released a sigh and turned back toward me. "You've done what you could for him, lass." The ghost of a grin spread across his lips. "Do you still want the bath?"

I couldn't help but nod. When I'd awakened from unconsciousness, Dougal had been there for me. We'd made love, and he brought me to new heights of pleasure. We also became intimately acquainted with the fancy Jacuzzi bathtub that could easily fit three or four humans...or one big, scary werewolf. The perks of being mated to the Alpha of the Scottish Pack.

"Aye, a bath sounds delish." I wrapped my arms around his waist, bringing him back to me and drawing in his musky lupine scent. "Thanks for the talk. I wish I could've spoken with him before he took off. It would've made me feel better about him going."

"Love, I talked with him." He trailed his fingertips over my back in light, soothing strokes. "If I weren't confident that he presented no danger to others, I wouldn't have let him go. He would've stayed here whether he favored the idea or not." The muscles in his lower back tensed beneath my touch, and his hand paused over my spine.

Something didn't feel right. I lifted my gaze to meet Dougal's. Was he not telling me something? We hadn't known each other for long, but my sharp, feline instincts knew when someone spoke an untruth. He wasn't outright lying, but he was holding something back. What could it be?

I bit my lower lip, regretting it as my teeth sank into one of the nearly healed spots where Alistair had punched me in the face. Instead of confronting Dougal, I turned my attention toward the window. "You would tell me if he was dangerous to himself, wouldn't you?"

"Aye, I would." His tone of voice wasn't as convincing as I'd wanted. He leaned away, putting me at arm's length. "Enough of that, I suppose. I'll draw the bath for you." Without another word, he strode to the en-suite bathroom. His hands clenched and unclenched at his sides all the way. The door snapped shut behind him, and he started the water running a few moments later.

Nausea churned inside me, and I held my stomach. Should I believe Dougal? Something about his words didn't feel right. The Jacuzzi tub would take a few minutes to fill, and I needed to get out of this bloody bedroom and away from him. The strain of standing there and trying to keep myself calm was becoming too much.

My stomach growled, and I glanced up at the round wrought-iron clock on the wall. It was almost one o'clock in the afternoon.

Many of the werewolves didn't like that their Alpha was mating with a wereleopard, so I usually skipped the mealtime rushes to keep my distance. It wasn't easy, because several of the wolves lived here in this honest-to-God castle full time. Apparently, that was how many Packs operated. The thought boggled my mind. How did they stand to be around one another all the time? How would I survive being the sole feline in this house full of wolves?

Every urge for solitude within me roared to run as fast and as far away from this place as I could. Too much held me here, though. Besides, if Colin returned from his trip, I wanted to be around to greet him. Maybe throttle him, too, but it'd be a greeting nonetheless...

I slid my leather jacket on over the white tank top, not wanting to reveal too much bruised skin, then headed for the kitchen to grab leftovers. Dougal had tried to convince me to eat with him and everyone else. He wanted me to get to know the wolves and socialize. Getting friendly with the Pack might be a nice idea, but I couldn't do it. Not with how his Pack watched me when they thought I wasn't looking. Even Dougal's second-in-command wasn't a fan of mine. The sentiment was mutual. For as long as I could remember, I'd hated werewolves. One of my main reasons would soon rest six feet underground. Their hatred of me for Alistair's death just added to my reluctance to get friendly with them.

Shaking away those thoughts, I turned the corner to enter the kitchen. If my sharp feline reflexes hadn't kicked in, I would've run straight into a towering werewolf. I leapt back at the last minute to prevent Kerr from spilling his plate of food. The already agonizing ache in my side intensified from moving so fast, but I kept my arms at my sides and my face neutral.

"Afternoon, lass. Ye look like yer recoverin' well." Kerr nodded, looking curiously at me.

"Thanks, Kerr. I'm trying." I flashed him an uncomfortable smile, then edged past the broad, barrel-chested man into the kitchen. Maybe he wasn't as bad as the others, but I couldn't shake the overwhelming feeling that he disagreed with Dougal's decision to mate with me.

Kerr placed a heavy hand on my shoulder. My spine stiffened, and I gripped the sleeves of my jacket to keep from swinging on him too. "Keep tryin', then." His deep voice rumbled through the kitchen. I glanced pointedly at his hand, but he didn't move it. "Sooner or later ye need to overcome yer fear, hatred, or whatever it is ye feel toward my kind. If ye cannae, ye won't last long here, lass." With that, he walked down the corridor toward the massive grand hall where the wolves held their meetings and ate.

My shoulders slumped. Suddenly, I didn't feel so hungry, but my leopard still needed to eat. We couldn't skip any more meals. It hindered our healing process and weakened us too much. Right now, I couldn't afford weakness, not while I was amongst a pack of wolves.

If only I weren't continually looking over my shoulder with the Pack, but such was life for now.

Shite. I didn't have much time before Dougal noticed I'd left the bedroom.

The leftovers were neatly arranged on the clean countertop. There wasn't much food left, but I grabbed a bag of crisps and one of the last club sandwiches. A female wolf —Mairi, I think—ran a catering company, so she always brought by food to keep the Pack well fed. She was one of the nicer wolves.

Instead of following Kerr toward the dining room, where

I would probably find the rowdy werewolves laughing and talking, I remained in the kitchen. I sat on the counter farthest away from the entrance, hidden from anyone who might walk past.

As I finished my sandwich, footsteps in the hall became louder as someone approached the kitchen. The sound of soft sniffing tensed every muscle in my body, then Dougal stepped into the room. His gaze slid over me, and desire darkened his eyes.

"Your bath is ready. If I'd known you were hungry, I would've brought something earlier when I ate."

I shrugged a shoulder. "It's all right. I'm eating now."

"Aye, so you are." He looked down the hallway as if checking to make sure no one else was near. When he turned back, he wore a frown that creased the corners of his lips and eyes. "You shouldn't be in here all alone, love. Things within the Pack are tense right now. Let's go back to the bedroom."

I tilted my chin up, not in the mood to be bossed around again. "I'm not alone. You're here." I opened the bag of crisps and munched on one.

His nostrils flared, and he crossed his arms over his broad chest. The move might've been scary as hell if it wasn't him doing it. "That's not the point. Come on."

Bloody hell.

First, I'd been his prisoner in the cage, and now I'd become a prisoner in his bedroom. Not in a fun way, either. Why was this happening?

I clenched my fists, crushing a few of my crisps as tears burned in my eyes, but I refused to let them show. The flood of emotions I'd experienced over the past week was becoming too much to all push down at once. As soon as I dealt with certain fears or emotions, others popped up to take their place, like some horrible version of whack-a-mole.

Life just wasn't fair. All I'd wanted to do was return to

Scotland and be here for my brother. In that time, I'd been reintroduced to a childhood nightmare, imprisoned in a dungeon, and now I was the prisoner/mate of a werewolf Alpha. When would the roller coaster end?

Dougal crossed the space between us in a few long strides. He pulled me from the counter into his arms.

A feline hiss ripped from my throat, sounding every bit as feral as I felt. Once again, anger rescued me from my moodiness. "Set me down this minute!"

2

DOUGAL

*W*omen were confusing as all bloody hell.

I wanted to be there for Caitlyn, to support her. Heaven knew she'd been through so much in her life. But the shame gripping at my chest was hard to shake. Alistair had been with the Scottish Pack for many years. His long-standing membership ultimately made him my responsibility. Perhaps if he'd been on a tighter leash, neither Alistair nor Duncan would be dead, and these bruises wouldn't still mar Caitlyn's body and mind. Colin leaving without saying goodbye deeply troubled her, and that was perfectly understandable. Her brooding and hiding away from the world made me realize there might be more to her unhappiness than just her brother's departure.

"Don't hiss at me. You can't show aggression like this." I put her back on the kitchen counter and cupped her face a wee bit forcefully as she struggled against me. "Stop! Don't do this where anyone could walk in and see. You're going to force me to assert my authority here. You can't act out toward me like this."

The threats went in one ear and out the other. She shook

her head. "Maybe I dinnae have what it takes to be with ye, then. Your Pack would be bloody thrilled if you chose someone else. Someone more befitting their Alpha." She shoved at my chest, trying to push past me with her bag of crisps.

Caitlyn's words cut me to the core. I could only handle so much right now. She had no idea the amount of pressure resting on my shoulders with the Pack's blatant displeasure. Dismissing my invitations to get to know the Pack didn't make things easier.

I tore the crisps away from her. The bag popped beneath my firm grip, raining crisps across the kitchen floor. Her saucy attitude was the last thing I needed. How could she say those words to me? The way we'd connected made me believe we both cared for one another. Being mates wasn't instant love, but it meant something. Maybe her feline kin didn't share those sentiments. The urge to grab her by the shoulders and firmly shake her nearly took over, but I choked it down. I'd promised her brother I would take care of her while he was gone, and I intended to do just that, even if she was making it incredibly difficult for me.

Caitlyn's eyes widened with shock as she looked between me and the crisps littering the floor. "Wha…"

"Looks like romance is in full swing here," Kerr said as he walked into the kitchen. Crisps crunched under his boots as he set his plate into the sink. He glanced between us, but when his gaze landed on Caitlyn, something seemed to pass between them.

Caitlyn froze and averted her gaze. The desire to grab her and shake her resurfaced. She'd screwed up by looking away. She was my mate now. If she wanted to be respected within the Pack, she had to act strong and with confidence like she was in charge. From what I'd seen, she was more than capable of behaving that way. Seeming unsure of herself and showing weakness would only undermine her position amongst the wolves.

"That it is. We're about to enjoy a bath, if there are no other comments about our love life." I couldn't help my biting tone, but Kerr had caught me at a time when I needed to be alone with my mate.

"Aye, laird. I'll leave ye to it, then." Kerr glanced at Caitlyn once more before dipping his head to me and then walking away.

I said nothing else, just hefted Caitlyn into my arms. I was careful of her injuries, but I kept a firm grip on her. She wouldn't race off without us finishing this conversation. Surprisingly, just as quickly as her temper had flared, she'd gone quiet and almost docile. This wasn't like her. Something had passed between my mate and my second-in-command. What was it, though?

The walk back to the bedroom felt longer than it should have. When we reached our room, I kicked the door closed behind us and carried her inside. A frown curved my lips as I set her to her feet. "Do you want to tell me what's going on between you and Kerr? Something changed when he walked into the room."

Caitlyn refused to meet my gaze, so I tilted her chin up to look me in the eyes. This time she didn't fight me, but she didn't answer my question either, as if I'd leave her alone if she didn't speak. Apparently, she hadn't yet learned that I never gave up on someone I cared about.

"I know something is wrong, love. If you don't let me in, I can't help with whatever is going on." I brushed my thumb over her cheek.

Exhaling a sigh, she lowered her gaze again. "What makes ye think I need your help with anything? Ye dinnae ken me. I've been taking care of myself since I was a lass. No one has ever been there to swoop in for my rescue."

"Maybe someone should've been." The words tumbled out before I could hold them back. "If they had, you wouldn't have suffered so much. Self-reliance is good, but not at the expense of your innocence."

Her lower lip quivered, and she sank her teeth into it, heedless of the cut there. Caitlyn shook her head. "It's too late to think that way. The only thing it'll do is stir up regret. I cannae change my past, even if I really want to."

"Nae, you can't, but you can get out of your own way when it comes to your future."

"Perhaps." She shrugged her shoulders and looked into my eyes, this time of her own accord. "Ye were saying about that bath?" She glanced toward the bathroom door likely looking for an escape from the conversation. It would be just as well to let her relax in the tub. I'd pressed her hard enough.

"Aye, I did. If you need anything, let me know. I can bring you more food, if you'd like." I placed my hand on her shoulder. "I'm sorry about the crisps. My temper ran away with me." I slid my hand down her arm and let it fall back to my side.

"Thanks." Her gaze returned to me, and she gave the ghost of a smile. "I wouldn't mind something more to eat." She walked toward the bathroom but paused when she reached the door. "It wasn't all your fault. I know you're trying to help. With everything that's happened…and then Colin leaving…my abandonment issues are flaring up." Without another word, she shut the door behind her. The soft thump of her clothes hitting the tiles and the slosh of water as she climbed into the tub made me want to join her.

But she needed her space, and I had to respect that.

My heightened senses took in every splash as Caitlyn bathed. I sat on the bed, not wanting to look away from the door. She was too hard on herself. If the lass didn't talk with someone, even her brother, she'd only prolong her suffering. That was the last thing I wanted for her.

The sting of her words still bothered me. Right now I needed to make sure she didn't push me away. I didn't know what I'd do if I lost my mate just after finding her. Life wouldn't be the same.

Something bothered me about the interaction between her and Kerr. It led me to believe she was being influenced to pull away from me. If she wouldn't say what was going on, then I needed to talk with Kerr. Unlike her, he wouldn't have a choice about whether he wanted to explain or not.

I strode from the bedroom and locked the door behind me, not comfortable leaving her vulnerable in a house full of wolves, especially if something sinister was happening behind my back. While there'd been whispers about the Pack being unhappy with me for entangling myself with a wereleopard, Caitlyn wasn't just a wereleopard to me. She was my *mate*. A wolf didn't choose those kinds of things. The road ahead of us might not be easy, but my wolf recognized her as mine.

It didn't take long for me to find Kerr in one of the sitting areas overlooking a small loch. Like the rest of the house, the room had a masculine tone, decorated in brown and cream colors along with dark, rich wood.

He climbed to his feet as I entered the room. "I figured ye'd come find me, laird."

"Why? Is there something you wish to say?"

With the other wolves, I could assert my dominance and use my position as Alpha to bring them in line. That worked to a certain extent with Kerr. As my second-in-command, he was one of the strongest wolves in the Pack. If he didn't want to deal with my shite, he could very well challenge me. The last thing this Pack needed was more turmoil, especially with the recent deaths and Caitlyn's presence. I didn't want this community of wolves to fracture even more or for a wolf to go rogue. That bloody well wouldn't be good for anyone, particularly the humans who got in my wolves' way if they lost their humanity.

Kerr nodded and returned to sitting on the sofa. "Aye, there is. As yer well aware, the funeral for Duncan and Alistair are tomorrow."

I clenched my fists at just hearing Duncan's name again. He'd been an omega wolf, the most subordinate of the Pack. I'd relied on him for advice, and he'd tried to help find Alistair. Why had I let him do that? Sure, he was partially responsible for Caitlyn being brutally attacked, but if I'd been a better Alpha, he wouldn't be dead. "Aye, I'm aware. What's your point?"

"Yer woman shouldn't plan on attendin'. Might put a strain on Pack members to see her there." Kerr glanced up at me as if checking to see whether he still held my attention. He knew he did, and I couldn't say I disagreed.

Caitlyn stubbornly refused to listen to reason. Try as I might to convince her that she shouldn't attend, she insisted on going both out of respect for her brother—regardless of how she felt about him right now—and for herself. Part of me admired her courage to attend the funeral, but I didn't understand why she'd want to put herself through that pain.

However, Kerr's motivations for talking about this with me now wasn't out of concern for Caitlyn's emotions. Instead, he believed it wasn't in the Pack's best interest to have her there. I should've been focused on the Pack's needs, as my father had taught me, but it was challenging not to think of Caitlyn's needs too. The two should've been fairly easy to balance, but for some reason, I was struggling.

"I'll talk with her about it," I said. Not like it would make a difference.

Kerr raised an eyebrow at me. "Laird, ye may want to do

more than talk to the lass. Ye need to be thinkin' of yer people. My advice is—"

"Kerr, I came here for information, not for your advice. If I wanted it, I'd ask." My tone was harsher than I'd intended, but for him to assume I wasn't thinking of my people? That infuriated me.

"Aye, that's so. However, I cannae impress on ye enough to open yer ears and listen to what our people need." He rose to his feet and crossed the room to stand in front of me. "I've been here for ye since yer da died, my laird. I dinnae ask much, but I have to ask this. Dinnae bring her. I implore ye. Lock her in the cage if necessary—"

My eyebrows shot up. Was he telling me to imprison her after what she'd suffered? How could he ask that? Caitlyn needed our help, not more punishment, especially not for wanting some closure and to be a good sister.

"Excuse me? I am listening to you. While I appreciate your backing, I can't lock her in the cage again. If attending the funeral means so much to her, I won't stand in her way. I can promise I'll try to make her see common sense. I am the Alpha of this Pack, and I stand with my kin. Nothing has changed in that regard. I care about my wolves, but she is my mate. I feel it in my soul, Kerr. Sooner or later, the Pack will have to accept that we're together now."

"Very well, laird. I understand ye have to do what's best for ye and the lass. Maybe the Pack would be more open to her if she wouldn't squirrel herself away in yer bedroom. Her current behavior hasn't helped the tension the wolves are feeling. I'm not denyin' that she's yer mate." His lips pressed together, and he shook his head. "The Pack needs to know yer still on their side too, especially after losing two of our members." Kerr bowed his head to me, then strode out of the room leaving me alone with the magnificent loch view and a heavy heart.

3

CAITLYN

*T*he warm bathwater soothed some of the aches and pains radiating through my body. Dougal had been right about soaking in the tub.

My agitation toward him fizzled a little. How could I remain upset? Besides, he was right about one thing. As the Alpha of the Pack, he had to appear strong. If his wolves saw his woman hissing at or arguing with him, their respect for him might be severely diminished. That could put us both in a lot of danger.

I sank deeper into the tub until only my eyes, nose, and mouth were above the water. What I needed most was to pull myself together and stop letting my emotions get the best of me. Once I did that, I'd be free to move past everything that had happened recently: trying to rescue Colin, Alistair's attack, and Colin leaving.

While I appreciated Dougal wanting to help, I'd never relied on anyone before in my life. It didn't come naturally to me. As a wereleopard, I was a solitary hunter not used to running in packs.

The soft creak of the bedroom door opening put me on edge, and I jerked upright in the tub, sloshing water around. With all the bubbles, no one would see my nudity. Nudity might not be a concern for many shifters, but being around the werewolves still made me nervous. To make things worse, I wasn't at my best physically or mentally right now.

"Caitlyn?" Dougal's voice eased my worries through the bathroom door. "I have the rest of your lunch."

"Give me a wee moment. I'm still in the bath." I grabbed a towel from the nearby rack and dried off. My clothes were standard-issue Pack sweats since I hadn't been able to bring the travel bag I'd left at Colin's place. Things had been hectic, so it was understandable, but I couldn't wait to have something of my own again.

Dougal was propped against the pillows on the bed when I walked into the bedroom. A big tray of food lay beside him on the king-sized bed. More food than I really wanted, but my hungry stomach growled all the same. He flipped through channels on the television protruding from the hideaway cabinet at the foot of the bed. When his gaze landed on me, he hopped up and set the remote aside.

"I'm fine. Dinnae get up for me." I waved my hand at him and pushed the food tray toward the foot of the bed so I could crawl beside him and eat. Eating in bed was almost becoming routine when I'd never done this before.

Silence stretched between us for a few minutes as we sat there—me eating another sandwich and some crisps while Dougal watched the telly. Unlike earlier, this moment was more peaceful and companionable, with no urgent need to break the silence.

Dougal glanced over at me every so often. Concern darkened his eyes, and the peace shattered. "We need to talk about tomorrow, love," he said.

What did we need to discuss? From the careful way he watched me, I doubted it'd be a pleasant topic. A heaviness settled in my chest. The funeral. The event hadn't strayed far from my thoughts. Maybe it was why I kept waiting for Colin to walk through the door. He wasn't a fan of his father now, but for most of his life, he hadn't known the man... This could be something he'd want to attend. A way of saying goodbye to the arse who helped bring him into the world.

Hell, that was one reason I wanted to go. To hopefully relieve my mind of its haunting nightmares by seeing that bastard lowered into the ground myself.

Although, if it had been my father—who I didn't know either—and if I were in his situation, I wouldn't be racing back here to attend the funeral. My da had never been present in my life, just like Alistair hadn't been present in Colin's. Perhaps for good reason, since they'd both abused our mother and her kids. Mum hadn't been able to pick nice, decent men—until now, at least.

"What about tomorrow?" I crunched on a crisp as I watched the news.

"You said before you wanted to go. Have you changed your mind?" The way he worded it so carefully set off alarm bells in my head. Of course he wanted me to change my mind. The Pack would be there, and he didn't want to piss them off. Too damn bad.

"Nae, I've not changed my mind. I'm still going." I pushed the tray between us and leaned back a little, trying to act casually. The last thing I wanted was to get into a big confrontation with him about this. As he'd said earlier, he didn't want me to dispute his position by arguing. I wouldn't argue, but I'd do what I wanted.

"Are you sure you're feeling up to it?" He shoved the tray down toward our feet again. "You're still recovering from—"

"Dinnae try to dissuade me. You'd just be wasting yer

breath." I frowned at him, then shook my head, turning my attention back to the telly. "Why are you even tryin' this?"

With a grimace, Dougal shut off the television and let it sink back into the cabinet. "It's not what's best for you, and it wouldn't be good for the Pack either. I don't want any conflict tomorrow. You should know I care about you and your feelings. You want to be there because you feel it's the right thing for him and for you, but do you really want to cause discomfort to so many others? It's not a good idea. End of story, love."

"Ye cannae just say 'end of story' like that." The words came out harsh, but I couldn't believe my ears. "We'll have to agree to disagree." Did someone put him up to this? I slid off the bed and pushed my feet into a pair of flip-flops. It didn't matter. I needed some fresh air and distance from him. "I'm going out. Dinnae wait up for me."

Dougal scrambled over the bed in the blink of an eye. If I hadn't been a wereleopard, I might not have seen him move. "Wait just a minute. Don't do this. You shouldn't be going out." His eyebrows drew together. He reached for me but stopped himself.

"Why? Why cannae I leave? If I'm not yer prisoner, I should be able to do as I wish—and that includes going out whenever I bloody well please!" I crossed my arms under my chest, and his gaze dipped to take in my breasts. Not what I was going for, but maybe it'd distract him from this futile argument.

"You...you're not a prisoner here. Don't be silly, love." He lifted his lusty gaze for a moment, and then his dark eyes lowered to my breasts again. "But that doesn't mean you can do whatever you wish or go out whenever you want. Even if this wasn't about the Pack—" He squeezed his eyes closed and gritted his teeth, as if furious with himself over fumbling and telling me a forbidden truth.

"*Och*, Kerr doesn't want me there." I should've known Kerr would pull something after the unnerving encounter I had with him earlier. Dougal was so worried about keeping his wolves happy that he didn't care about what I needed.

If that was how our relationship would be, then I didn't have the patience for it. I couldn't be with someone who needed to constantly please others like this. So many things about this relationship felt too constricting when my leopard and I so desperately craved a wee bit of freedom again.

I'd sleep at Colin's place tonight, go to the funeral tomorrow, then I'd contemplate our future together. Colin wasn't using his home, so it'd be somewhere to lay my head until I found a place of my own and a job to sustain me.

"Come on, Caitlyn." Dougal shook his head. "This isn't just about him. You're different. They have a hard time dealing with what they don't know, and you haven't tried to get to know them. They're uncertain about you. That's all." He nodded toward the bed. "Just lie down and relax, okay? Everything will be fine."

I scoffed. "It's hard for me to open up to them. A werewolf made my life a living hell, and most other wolves have been cruel to me throughout the years. My own brother has even been difficult to handle at times." This was all becoming too much for me. If I didn't leave soon, I might end up getting myself into more trouble than I'd bargained for. "Ye just dinnae understand."

Turning my back on Dougal, I walked to the bedroom door. Trying to explain my feelings to him was a waste of breath. I obviously wasn't getting through. His quiet footsteps followed me, and the hair on the back of my neck rose.

As I reached for the doorknob, he spun me around to face him and so gently pushed me against the door. He leaned in close until our foreheads were touching. "Please, love. I know you're upset. If it were only up to me, you could go—"

"It *is* up to ye. You're their Alpha." I pushed at his broad chest, but he held me firmly against the door. The more strength I put into my struggles, the less it felt like I was accomplishing anything. My breathing sped up, but my throat closed up tight. Helplessness rushed through me, and I was suddenly back in the cage with Alistair looming over me as he slammed his fists into my face. "Let me go," I said, my voice cracking and sounding weak—no, helpless—even to my own ears. Who was this person? I didn't know her.

"I cannae. I cannae let you attend the funeral. I cannae let you leave the house on your own." His brogue was much thicker than normal and had taken on a pleading tone I wasn't used to from Dougal. It almost frightened me. "You have to know it's not that simple. Hasn't your brother told you anything about how werewolf society operates?"

I nodded my head.

"I dinnae want to hold you back, and I dinnae understand why you need to attend the funeral, but I ken it matters to you. It's not all about what I think, though. The Pack isn't stable right now. Not after all that has happened both with the deaths and with me taking you as my mate. If I let you go and something happened to you, I'd never forgive myself."

My mouth dropped open, and I blinked up at Dougal. "Ye think one of your wolves would kill me?" Aside from Alistair, I hadn't considered that a real possibility. Of course I knew the Pack didn't like me or my presence here...but murdering me?

An icy chill slithered down my spine.

"Nae, not necessarily. Ah hell, I dinnae fucking ken. Maybe?" Leaning down, he placed a tender kiss against my lips that sent heat pooling between my legs, replacing the cold wisp of fear. "If you attempt to attend the funeral tomorrow, I'd be forced to lock you up. I'm sorry, love."

"Wh…what?" I searched his face, trying to see if he was joking, but what I saw showed he was deathly serious. "Are ye joking? Why the hell would ye do somethin' like that?" Hurt clenched at my chest. He would lock me up—possibly in the cage—for trying to attend the funeral? Why was I even lounging in his bedroom?

Tears burned behind my eyes, but I held them at bay. I refused to let him see me cry. Perhaps the spark I'd felt for him all along was some sort of mate bullshit, or maybe it'd all been physical. The full moon had risen not long before our first time. Perhaps all we had was just lust because of its influence.

"I'm not joking, love."

I leaned my head back against the door and looked up at the ceiling. The chances of him letting me walk out of here on my own were slim, especially now. He wouldn't want me to escape. But I'd figure out a way. If I could evade the research facility's trained mercenaries for several months, I could handle an Alpha and his dogs.

"Let me go." A token of werewolf knowledge came to me then. I lowered my gaze to stare directly into his eyes, knowing it was a challenge…daring him to do something. The only time I'd really looked into his eyes before was during sex.

He gritted his teeth, and his hands tensed on my shoulders until I was sure I'd have bruises afterward. "You have no idea the mistake you're making, love. Come to your senses by morning, for both of our sakes." He released me and took a few steps back before stalking into the bathroom.

Cold shock numbed my body, and I remained against the door for a few moments. A war waged within me. Had I done the right thing or just royally screwed up? I hoped some small part of me knew what I was doing.

The sound of glass shattering rang out from the bathroom, and I bit my lip hard to hold in a surprised cry. If I was leaving, the best time—maybe the only time—was now.

With that, I took off my flip-flops, carrying them in my hand, and stalked out of the house before beginning the long walk back to civilization.

4

DOUGAL

*B*lood flowed freely from my hand as I held it over the sink. Punching the mirror hadn't been smart, but blazing hot anger had driven me over the edge. If I'd been stronger, I would have locked Caitlyn in the cage as Kerr suggested, but the look on her face when I even mentioned it nearly shattered my heart. If I hadn't lost my patience and been weak, she would still be with me now.

Perhaps the Pack was right. Maybe I was pussy-whipped. Her saucy feline attitude rattled my nerves and melted my spine. The Pack weighed heavily on my shoulders since my brother had refused to claim the Alpha title after our father died. The position wasn't easy before Caitlyn, but ever since she came into my life, I felt like I was failing miserably.

I pulled the larger shards of glass from my palm and dropped them into the sink, then wrapped a towel around my palm. The smaller pieces still grated under my skin like sandpaper. The Pack's doctor, Roy, would have one more reason to shake his head at me. *What a wanker.* Before I could leave the room, a rapid knock sounded on the door.

"What?" I shouted, not happy with the interruption.

"Laird, Lyall noticed your mate on the road to Edinburgh and brought her back for you," Hendrie, one of the younger and more loyal wolves, said from behind the door. "He told me she wasn't keen on returning. Nevertheless, she's awaiting you in the grand hall with Lyall and Kerr watching over her."

Bloody fucking fuck.

I clenched my hands into fists, not caring about the sharp pain shooting up my arm from breaking the mirror. "Have her brought to my chambers along with the doctor. I'll deal with her here." After our last conversation, I wasn't looking forward to talking with her, but I *really* didn't want to argue with Kerr about her behavior in front of the Pack. He'd give me that cocky knowing look that said I told you so.

"My apologies, laird, but Kerr requests you join them in the grand hall. He'd prefer to talk with you both there."

I jerked the bedroom door open and glared at Hendrie. "Is Kerr your Alpha, or am I?" Brushing off my second-in-command would likely carry ramifications, but I couldn't think about that. Right now, my number one concern was deciding what to do with Caitlyn. Numbness slid over me, stealing some of my anger. I didn't want to be bothered. If it were up to me, I would've had Lyall just let her walk to Edinburgh to blow off some steam.

Even as my mind constructed that thought, pain squeezed my chest. How could I think that? I pushed the emotion away, focusing again on the numbness.

Hendrie stared at me with wide eyes as if unsure what to do. He dropped his gaze to the floor after a few seconds. On the way down, his eyes caught on the towel wrapped around my hand. "S-sorry, laird. I'll fetch your mate and the Pack doctor at once. My apologies." He kept his head bowed as he backed down the hall a few steps before rushing off to the grand hall.

I snapped the door shut, then leaned against the sturdy oak. A crimson stain spread out over the once cream-colored towel, and the small shards of glass embedded in my hand were a solemn reminder of my stupidity. I cursed under my breath.

Caitlyn had a way of bringing out the best and the worst in me. For the love of all that was holy, I wished she would pick one.

Now the decision was out of my hands. I'd tried to shelter her, but it didn't matter what I did now. She'd have to go to the cage. If I did nothing else, I needed to do that. Pack members were held to a certain standard, and she'd crossed the line. As my mate, she carried the rank of an honorary Pack member, even if some of the Pack wished she wasn't.

Footsteps approached the bedroom door, but I waited for Hendrie's knock. "Laird, I've brought your mate. I also informed the doctor of your injury, and he's on his way over."

Roy didn't live on the premises. During the day, he had a normal medical practice just outside of Edinburgh. Living here would've looked suspicious on all the government forms that came with being a doctor, and the last thing we wanted was to draw more attention to ourselves. Besides, Roy was a cranky old wolf who enjoyed his own space. It was better for everyone if he wasn't here all the time.

"Cheers, Hendrie."

Hendrie and Caitlyn stood side by side when I opened the door. He held her by the elbow. The furious scowl she aimed at the young wolf was threatening, as if she could tear his throat out if he didn't release her. I didn't doubt that. She was strong. Was she allowing Hendrie to guide her around because she didn't want the Pack to descend on her?

While I was frustrated by what happened, I didn't want my wolves to injure her.

I reached for Caitlyn, and she stiffened. It hurt seeing her react like that toward me. Her gaze dropped to the towel wrapping my hand, and tension tightened the corners of her eyes. I pushed her behind me, a few steps farther into the bedroom. "Let me know when the doc arrives."

"Aye, laird. I will." Hendrie bowed his head and began his backward walk again.

I closed the door, not caring about proper etiquette at this point. Nothing would please me more than having this evening end already. Tension radiated through my shoulders, and I didn't turn to face Caitlyn for several moments. Instead, I focused on my breathing, trying to regain control of my beast, who relentlessly pushed toward the surface of my skin.

"You know what's going to happen. It can't be helped now. You're upset with me, but I asked you not to leave. You shouldn't have taken off." My tone was emotionless, and I wrapped myself in the dominance of an Alpha wolf, trying to imitate how strong and commanding my father was when faced with wolves who didn't follow Pack protocol. He never let his anger take hold and make him aggressive toward his people. He'd always maintained a cool, calm demeanor when he dished out punishment.

"I'm not one of ye. Yer wolves cannae drag me around like I am." Caitlyn didn't even sound angry anymore, just tired and utterly frustrated. "If my brother were here—"

"Colin might talk some sense into your thick skull." I whirled on her. "He might also be in greater danger because you couldn't keep a cool head and listen to what I fucking said. I'm *not* against you, love. I care about you deeply, in ways I've never cared for another woman before, but I can't stand by while you're reckless and apt to start trouble within my Pack. I'm already putting my people in danger by creating a divisive environment. You wouldn't understand that, though." Somewhere during my speech, frustration crept back into my voice. What did it matter? The woman was as stubborn as her brother, if not more so.

The blood-soaked towel needed to be changed out if I didn't want blood drops on the floor. I headed for the bathroom to get another one. Judging by all the bleeding, I'd likely nicked an artery.

Surprisingly, Caitlyn followed me into the bathroom. "How can I help with yer hand?" Her voice had softened from the aggressive tone she'd used before we parted.

I took a deep breath, then released it, slowly trying to relax. "Another towel from the cabinet would be great."

Without hesitation, she brought me a new cream-colored towel. She placed it beside me and then sat on the counter. Concern filled her gaze as she watched me, but she kept quiet.

I couldn't look at her. If I did, my emotions would continue to fluctuate, and I wanted to keep my cool anger around me like a protective blanket. She'd hurt me worse than I'd been hurt in a long time. Perhaps ever since my brother ran off. I shook the thought away as I tossed the bloody towel in the sink with the shards of mirror, then pressed the clean cloth against my hand.

A brief knock thumped against the bedroom door before it opened without waiting, and Roy, the Pack doctor, strode into the bathroom. Disdain wrinkled his nose when he noticed Caitlyn's presence. Then he set his bag on the counter and began tending to my hand.

My heart ached for my mate again. Everyone was so ready to push her away. Had I been too harsh with her earlier? I didn't know how to balance having a feline mate in a wolf Pack. "Caitlyn, wait for me in the bedroom. Watch television if you want. This shouldn't take long."

She opened her mouth to respond, but at the last minute,

she nodded. Not long after her leaving, a broadcaster on the telly began reciting the news before Caitlyn flipped through the channels.

"This wasn't entirely her fault," I said to Roy. "And I don't like seeing you look at my mate like that."

Roy glowered at me before lowering his gaze. "Lad, this *is* her fault. She upset you, causing you to react foolishly. Here I am tending to you when I could be enjoying supper with my wife." He shook his head as he worked on cleaning the wounds, plucking the rest of the shards from my hand before they became permanently embedded. "If you could've found someone else, even a human, you wouldn't be having such a fuss here. Instead, you get yourself enamored by a kitty cat."

I slammed my uninjured fist against the counter and growled low in my throat. "Do *not* question my choice of mate. As many wolves before me have witnessed, finding your true mate is an almost metaphysical experience. I cannae tell my wolf, or my heart, who to choose. You and the Pack dinnae have any right in telling me who I can mate."

Roy scowled at me. Deep lines creased his wrinkly forehead. "No, the Pack can't tell you who to mate. That much is true. They can decide whether or not they want you as their Alpha, though. Rumors have been going around about a challenge. No one has the gall or the strength to do it. Yet. You and I both know a couple people in the Pack who could pose a threat to your leadership if a challenge were called." He plucked the last piece of glass from my hand, then set the tweezers on the counter. "I'm on your side, lad, whether you believe it or not. Your father was a damn good man, and a great Alpha. When the position fell upon your shoulders, I might not have been the most compassionate since I'd lost a friend. But I've been your loyal wolf." He grabbed my shoulders and shook me. "Don't let what your father worked hard for come crashing down because of *her*. I couldn't bear it." He released me, cleansed the wounds again, then wrapped the hand in gauze.

Silence stretched between us.

For so long, I'd thought Roy didn't like me. I'd taken his crabby behavior as disapproval that the Alpha's youngest brat was now the laird. Never had I imagined that maybe his reactions were due to deeper, more personal reasons.

"I'm sorry I misunderstood you," I said finally. "I never stopped to think about how my father's passing may have affected you."

Roy waved away my apology with a flick of his wrist. "Don't worry about that, lad. If you want to do something for me, watch your back. Don't let your prick steal your common sense." He patted me on the back, then nodded to my hand. "Should be healed soon, now that the glass is out and it's clean. Your father restored this castle as a nice headquarters for the Pack, don't go all half-cocked and wreck it, or your body."

I nodded, feeling a little sheepish, like a young lad in trouble over doing something stupid. "Aye, cheers."

He left the room and closed the door behind him.

But I couldn't hide in the bathroom forever. The thought of returning to Caitlyn's side after what had passed between us made me want to get some fresh air. She'd dealt with a lot even before Alistair stumbled upon her at Colin's house. While I wanted to remain furious with her—and fuck was I ever—she wasn't the only one to blame for this mess.

Things were precarious right now. If I made one wrong move, all the tension between the Pack and Caitlyn could blow up in my face like nothing I'd ever experienced.

Tomorrow's funeral felt like a make-or-break moment. The event could allow me to cement the Pack's loyalty once more…or I could end up losing everything.

5

CAITLYN

*D*ougal remained on his side of the king-sized bed as if a stream of lava divided the mattress. Not being close to him exacerbated the pressure clenching my chest. How were we supposed to present a united front for the Pack, if we couldn't share a bed without this gaping pit between us? I stared at the ceiling as the grandfather clock in the corner ticked off the minutes. Sleep wouldn't come, no matter how hard I tried. The room slowly grew brighter as the sun finally rose.

I controlled my breathing and closed my eyes as Dougal stirred, not wanting him to know I was awake. Hopefully, he'd go to the funeral and allow me to find my own way. The Pack's HQ had a few back-up vehicles in case of emergency. If they weren't all taken, I might be able to borrow one. This time, I'd be careful and not expect to be allowed to walk off into the sunset.

My teeth clenched at the thought of staying here, and I considered going back to Colin's apartment once the funeral was over. I'd attend the ceremony, then I could take off and rebuild my life away from the reach of the angry pack of wolves breathing down my neck.

No, I still cared about Dougal, even if what was happening upset me. I didn't want our newly formed relationship to end before we'd even had a chance to explore it. Dougal had protected me and my brother from Alistair's shite. Colin had been ready to escape and get me out of the cage. What would've happened if it went down that way? Could it have been Colin who died instead of Alistair and Duncan? Nausea churned in my stomach at the thought of Colin's name on a headstone, and the urge to vomit grew stronger.

Rolling to my side, I clenched my belly as I pushed those thoughts from my mind. My breathing came out in short, quick pants, and I worked to normalize it again. It was hard with the heavy weight of that burden.

Colin had returned to Scotland for peace, all while dealing with his beast. Instead, he'd discovered the monster his father truly was and that the man he'd fondly thought of growing up didn't exist. He'd heard a tall tale our mother spun so reality wouldn't dash Colin's innocence. Our mother had been more open with me. She'd sheltered me from my father, but that hadn't stopped her from finding another man.

Dougal ran his hand over my sweat-slick back, and I let out a soft sigh, feeling less alone. He covered my shoulders with the blanket as if I'd catch a cold. The kind gesture calmed my fears that our relationship might be irreparably damaged, but it also reinforced the importance of being stealthy if I didn't want him to hate me later. He rolled me onto my back, and I blinked up at him. I hadn't slept much, and judging by the dark circles under his eyes, I guessed he hadn't either.

"You're staying home, right?" The carefulness in his voice

made me nervous. He leaned closer but kept his hand on my shoulder, his thumb caressing against my skin.

I nodded, not wanting to lie to him, but his hand distracted me when I needed to sound convincing.

Maybe he noticed since his hand lightly clenched, almost like a warning. "Say the words. I don't want to lock you up after what you went through." He paused, his thumb stroking my neck. "I need to know you'll be here when I get back, that you won't go against me. My reputation with the Pack can't afford it, love."

"I'll stay home." The words scratched my throat as they came out. "I wish I could be there to comfort you." Even if that wasn't my primary motive for attending, I knew how much the deaths bothered him, and I wanted to be there for him.

He pulled back and sat on the bed facing away from me. His head bowed down, and my heart broke bit by bit. "Aye, that wouldn't be prudent, though. If you want, I'll tell you what it's like."

"I'd like that." I balled my hands into fists under the sheets. *Fuck.* Lying to Dougal sucked hard. I could kick myself for what I was going to do, especially after he was this gentle and kind to me. He deserved better. I hated how I couldn't be the mate his Pack needed after everything we'd been through. Memories of last night came to mind when I lashed out at him, walked away, and he ended up fighting with a mirror.

Dougal continued to sit there in silence, and I uncurled my fingers, wanting to comfort him at the start of what would likely be a sad, stressful day for him. His muscular back was tight, and I gently caressed my fingers over the warm expanse, kneading my thumb into a few of the knots to break them up. The bed creaked a little as he turned to face me. His intense gaze seared my insides, spreading heat through my thighs.

I pushed to my knees and closed the gap between us. Whatever had happened before faded away in that moment. None of that mattered, only this shared experience with the man I cared about. I wrapped my arms around his neck as my lips brushed against his, putting every ounce of tenderness and emotion I possessed into the kiss. No one had ever made me feel loved before. Maybe I needed to tame my rebellious side to ensure that didn't fade.

Dougal froze for a moment as if unsure how to react, then tugged me into his lap. He deepened our kiss as if equally desperate for this. His hands ran down my back to cup my arse, pulling me closer to him. The press of his hard cock against my belly made me gasp. The last time we'd enjoyed one another was a couple days ago. Too many messy emotions and hurt feelings, particularly on my part, had ruined any chance for romance.

Maybe this intimacy would help resolve some of our issues. Maybe I could back down and submit to his orders like a Pack mate would. But my leopard hissed in rejection at the idea of being robbed of our voice. Regardless, the hussy wanted this connection with Dougal and his beast almost as much as I did.

I lifted my hips a little and pushed the front of his pajama bottoms down. With that accomplished, I started to strip off my underwear, but Dougal's continued hold on my arse made it challenging.

"*Och*, love, you're feeling randy?" Dougal raised an eyebrow, amusement sparkling in his eyes. He glanced at the grandfather clock and grinned at me. "Sadly, we only have time for a quickie before I need to get a shower and dress." He kept one hand on my backside while his other slid beneath my t-shirt and ripped my panties off. "That's how it's done."

A gasp erupted from my throat at the sudden action, and I stared at him with wide eyes. This was the man that both intimidated and thrilled me when we'd first met. Moisture dampened my thighs. His finger pressed inside my core, drawing a low moan from my lips, and I ground against his hand. I wanted so much more than his fingers.

"Bloody hell. You're so wet and ready for me." Dougal's voice was a deep rumble. He kept rocking his finger into me as he pressed kisses along my neck. His body was almost vibrating with lust. My beast purred inside my chest, and only when Dougal chuckled did I realize I could hear it with my ears too.

My core clenched as his finger brushed the small pea-sized bundle of sensitive nerves inside me. "Dougal," I cried out, throwing my head back. My fingernails dug into his shoulders, and desire burned white-hot within me. "Stop. I *need* you."

He slowly withdrew his finger, then twirled us around so I lay flat on my back. His blue eyes were now the smoldering amber of his wolf. My breath caught in my throat at the sight. The press of his thick cock at my entrance brought another moan to my lips. Inch by blessed inch, he pushed inside me.

The first time we'd had sex, he'd treated me like a fragile human, but we quickly remedied that. Now he made love to me like we were equals. I could handle the real him and his beast.

I spread my legs wider, wanting to take all of him... wanting all he had to offer.

Dougal watched me with those scorching wolf-amber eyes. He slowly pulled out until only the tip of his dick was inside, only to drive himself fully into me, and then he did it again. The delicious sensations made me want more—from the slight twitch of his lips, I could tell that was the response he wanted to elicit.

"Tease," I gasped.

"Aye, love, but I'm only a tease if I don't deliver...and I always do."

Two could play at that game. I clenched the muscles in my core around his cock in between each stroke.

He let out a groan of pleasure and froze there, then his gaze lifted to meet mine. Desire erased every other emotion there, and he gripped my hips, thrusting into me as if he was trying to make me one with the mattress. The intensity nearly stole my breath.

My climax drew closer as he bucked his hips wildly. My back arched again as wave after wave of pleasure swept over me. I cried out, bunching the sheets in my fists. The soft sounds of fabric ripping did nothing to mask Dougal's groans of pleasure, which intensified as he released his hot cum inside me.

Dougal rolled onto the bed beside me, pulling me into his arms. We stayed like that for a few moments, until the grandfather clock chimed. "I hate to leave you after that beautiful moment, love, but I've got to prepare for the funeral." He slid his hand along my side toward my hip. "Perhaps after the wake, we can continue this?"

Heat warmed my insides at his suggestion of a round two, and I nodded. My wereleopard purred in agreement. "Aye, ye know where to find me."

A twinge of guilt hit me. We might not get a chance to pick this back up if I followed my heart and attended the funeral against his wishes. Maybe I should accept what the Pack wanted and stay behind?

*A*fter Dougal left that morning, my mind wouldn't shut up. I'd told him I would remain at home—and for a few moments, I'd believed I would—but I couldn't do it. I wouldn't be able to live with myself if I didn't do this. Almost all of the Pack had gone to the funeral, so their HQ was a ghost town. It was fairly easy to find where they kept the keys to the spare vehicles.

I parked a little way off from the cemetery and legged it so no one would be suspicious. So far, so good.

I stalked closer to the funeral, taking cover behind a tall oak tree. The large group of wolves wouldn't be happy if I disturbed them, and my sense of hearing was excellent, so I didn't need to be close to know what was going on.

Dougal stood in a kilt among his wolves. They all had their heads bowed and were talking low amongst themselves as if they were in a library. My heart ached for their loss, although I wasn't sad Alistair was dead. He got what he deserved.

The other wolf, though, Duncan... If Alistair hadn't been allowed to get so out of control, he might still be alive. He didn't seem like a bad guy. Just a wolf in the wrong place at the wrong time.

The funeral progressed for quite a while, and no one seemed to particularly notice me. I'd gotten better at hiding from my enemies after the research laboratory experience. When the service was about to end, I turned to leave my hiding spot, but two wolves were already heading toward me. The wind must have changed directions while I wasn't paying attention.

I lengthened my stride, but they had longer legs. It would draw too much attention if I took off running. I needed to keep my cool and keep walking. If all went well, they wouldn't want to make a big scene, and I could slip away without the entire Pack knowing I'd been there. Except one of those two wolves was Kerr.

My stomach somersaulted, and I took even breaths to calm myself. The other wolf was an older guy whom I didn't know. With a quick glance at the rest of the Pack, I saw that Dougal still wasn't aware of my presence. He was conversing with the others who were standing closer to the graves.

Kerr caught my eye again, and put his palm up, signaling me to stop. Maybe I should wait and hear what he had to say. I'd have to deal with them sooner or later. If I ran, I'd only be making things worse for myself later.

"Caitlyn," Kerr said as he drew near.

"Kerr." I nodded at him as I leaned against a thick tree, using it as cover against the rest of the group. "What do ye want? I was just—"

"Yer not allowed here, lass." He crossed his arms over his broad chest. His Argyll jacket groaned a little as his huge muscles flexed. If he kept trying to show off, he'd have to buy a new one. It was the first time i'd noticed how powerful he was.

"Aye. But Scotland is a free country, last I checked." It was a smarmy, smart-ass reply, but I didn't give a shite. I wanted to leave before Dougal noticed me. "I'm on my way now. Just let me go."

"Nae, 'tis too late now, lass." He took a step toward me, but he didn't reach for me. "Come along now. Ye are my laird's mate, and I don't wish to harm ye. Dougal will have me neck, so dinnae force me to do something that will cause us both a world of trouble."

The older wolf who'd come with him crept forward and edged toward my side. The bastard was trying to blockade me in, so I'd be stuck between them and the tree. If I stepped back, I'd reveal my presence to the group, especially now that Kerr was confronting me. I doubted the other wolves would remain oblivious for long. They might be dull at times, but they weren't entirely stupid, unfortunately. I rolled my eyes.

I held up my hands but didn't back down from either of them. Dougal had warned me not to show weakness in front of the Pack, so I wouldn't, even if it got me in trouble…again. "Dinnae take a step closer. Either of you."

"Ye don't get to talk, bitch," the older wolf growled. He took another step toward me, but Kerr shoved him back.

"Dinnae call my mate a bitch." The deep, rumbling voice behind me suddenly almost made me climb the tree.

The older wolf's upper lip trembled, baring a hint of his pointed teeth. He must have spent plenty of time in wolf form for his teeth to be so wolfishly sharp. "She can't just muck about in our business. It's not right, laird. This funeral doesn't concern her! She's the cause of Alistair's and Duncan's deaths. If she hadn't come around, neither of our wolves would be in the ground now."

"Duncan isn't dead because of me!" Fury sent my blood boiling, and I squeezed my hands into fists. "Y—"

The older wolf's meaty fist slammed into my jaw, snapping my head back and sending me spiraling into the tree with an *oomph*. My vision faded slightly, but I pushed to my feet and launched myself at him. We fell to the ground with me straddling his chest. I fired off two punches before strong arms pulled me away. Moisture trickled down my neck and back, and my cheek hurt.

Loud yells erupted around me. Pack members were fighting either for Dougal or against me. At least some of the wolves were loyal to their Alpha and didn't hate my guts, though it was tough to tell how many were on our side with the tangle of snarling bodies.

I squirmed against the arms restraining me, wanting to get back into the fight. Dougal didn't need a mate who pulled her punches, and lucky for him, that'd never be me.

Dougal dragged me away from the others. He shook me and grabbed my chin between his calloused fingers. "Stop fighting me!"

I gritted my teeth and pushed against his chest. "Aye, fine. Let me go."

His touch lingered for longer than I liked just then, and I didn't think he'd release me, especially with all the fighting around us. If someone else decked me, I'd be a sitting duck. "What the shite are you doing here? I thought we agreed you'd stay home." He shook his head, but pushed me behind him, away from the frenzied mob of werewolves.

"We talked about it, but I couldn't. I cannae say I'm sorry, because you know how I felt. But I am sorry I've caused this madness." I placed a hand on his back, almost expecting him to shrug it off, but he surprised me.

"Next time, I'll follow my instincts and lock you up." He shot me a warning look over his shoulder, and we navigated toward Kerr, who was trying to break up some of the werewolves. "Stop fighting, lads," Dougal shouted. "Cut the shite! This is a cemetery, for Christ's sake."

Two men took longer to settle down than the rest, but they were all restless, looking ready to brawl again at any moment.

My stomach jittered, and I kept my hands at my sides. I didn't want to do anything that would draw attention, even if what I really wanted was to place my hands over my churning stomach and curl up beneath Dougal's warm blankets in his room. That would be a helluva lot more peaceful than what I'd rained down upon us.

"Your whore is the reason our men are dead." One of the men toward the back bellowed the words, and the hair on the back of my neck rose. If I'd seen who had spoken, I would have torn his throat out.

"Dinnae call yer laird's mate a whore," Kerr shouted.

Dougal's back vibrated with rage. If we didn't get out of there soon, he'd lose his cool, and I'd be the one holding *him* back. "I'll take it from here, laird. Get the lass on back home."

Something about how Kerr said that made me want to run as fast and as far as my legs could take me. It sounded as if he expected Dougal would punish me. This time, I probably wouldn't blame him if he did.

Dougal nodded, then turned and placed his hand on the small of my back, half-guiding and half-shoving me toward the parking lot. Another wolf escorted us. It seemed like Dougal had his own chauffeur. It wouldn't surprise me.

6

DOUGAL

*G*ordon, the driver who walked with us, opened the black sedan's door for me and Caitlyn to slide in the back. When Caitlyn climbed in, I could sense his disapproval, but he diverted his gaze and closed the door behind us.

I seethed, my anger barely restrained beneath the surface. How could I have been stupid enough to believe she would stay home? Still, the fear of losing her churned in my gut. I dug my fingernails into my palms to keep my beast in check. She could've been killed if I hadn't intervened. My wolves carried far more resentment toward her than I'd imagined.

They didn't know the full scope of what happened with Alistair, and the fact he was Colin's da. How could I tell them the truth, especially knowing how he'd abused Caitlyn? They likely only saw him as a Pack member who was killed after a feline came around, but Alistair had wreaked hell on the siblings' lives. He wasn't the innocent one. However, if I did address this issue, it would tarnish his memory. I didn't want to do that to a longtime wolf with plenty of friends, particularly not when the Pack was on the verge of fracturing.

I glanced at Gordon as he sat in the driver's seat. Bloody hell, what was I doing to the Pack? How much longer could this go on before it broke irrevocably? Deep in my heart, regardless of our current problems, Caitlyn was mine. I'd never wanted another woman as my mate. How could I give her up to satisfy my wolves, whom I was supposed to lead and protect? My life was bigger than my day-to-day problems. The Pack needed me, but I was torn between my responsibility to my mate and to my kin.

Caitlyn leaned her head against the seat and closed her eyes. Her lips curved in displeasure. "I didn't mean for any of that to happen. I just..." She opened her eyes and gazed out the window. "I *needed* to be there. I *needed* to see Alistair's coffin lowered into the ground. After what he did to me as a child—let alone his recent abuse—I'd hoped attending the funeral would help erase the memories of him that plague me, and maybe allow me to sleep at night knowing he was truly gone. I'm sorry if ye cannae understand that."

The driver glanced at me in the rearview mirror before switching on the radio and returning his attention to the road. He couldn't miss our conversation, but at least he attempted to give us privacy.

Hearing Caitlyn's words hurt my heart. Memories of her opening up about her childhood in the cage came back to me. She hadn't gone against my wishes because of stubbornness. If only I'd known what the funeral meant to her. "You should've told me this yesterday, love. Do you realize you could've gotten yourself killed out there? I dinnae ken what I'd have done if that had happened." I pulled her chin toward me before caressing her cheek with my thumb. "You have no idea what you mean to me. I want you more than I've ever wanted anyone. If anything happened to you, I don't know what I'd do."

"You mean the world to me, too." She slid her tongue over her lower lip, and the desire to kiss her nearly drove me to press my lips to hers. "I didn't think talking would make a difference, especially when you mentioned the cage." Her gaze shifted from my eyes toward my lips. "To be fair, I...I was trying to avoid the crowd. I was going to leave before anyone noticed me, but I was a bit too late for that." She leaned her face into my palm, and I wrapped my other arm around her shoulders, drawing her closer. Having her close relaxed the raging beast inside me. She was safe...for now.

"Aye. That you were. I'm going to skelp your wee behind if you pull a stunt like that again." My voice cracked even as I tried to mask my panic at the thought of losing her.

Caitlyn widened her eyes as she wrapped her arms around me. A fine tremble rolled through her as she buried her face into my chest. She'd experienced things in life that no one should have to face. I wanted to make sure nothing bad ever happened to her again. My beast growled in protective approval.

The driver cleared his throat and lowered the radio's volume. "We're almost home, laird." His disapproving demeanor softened somewhat. He loved a human woman. Maybe he could understand how I felt more than the rest of the wolves. But one person's change of heart about my mate wouldn't matter in the end.

"Thank you, Gordon."

We rode in silence down the long driveway, with Caitlyn resting her head against my chest.

When I saw the front of my father's castle, my heart nearly leapt out of my chest. A large swath of Pack members stood with Kerr, who towered over all of them. He was in a shouting match with a few of the wolves, but they stopped what they were doing as the car came to a halt.

Caitlyn pulled away. For a moment, I could smell her fear before she shoved those emotions down. Smart lass.

I adjusted my Argyll jacket, fidgeting with the buttons as I waited for the driver to open my door. I needed to know what was going on. The events at the funeral must have sparked something much larger than I'd fathomed. When Gordon opened the door, the crowd lurched toward the car, but Kerr and Gordon and a handful of others held the majority at bay.

Bloody hell.

Caitlyn tried to squeeze out of the car behind me, but I blocked her exit. It was safer for her to stay where she was at the moment. She opened her mouth to argue, but then understanding flickered in her emerald-green eyes, and she closed the car door.

"What's the meaning of this?" I said, staring at Kerr.

He met my gaze for the span of a few heartbeats before dropping his. Something was wrong. He hunched his shoulders a little. "Laird, it's best if we speak in private."

"Tell him what you've let the rabble do," said Flora, one of our few female members, who was helping to hold back the crowd. She growled at Kerr. Anger flooded her scent, although I knew she was usually calm and pretty laid back. "Do it, or I will."

"This is not the time or place, Flora. Stand down." Kerr drew himself to his full height and narrowed his eyes at her. He was intimidating on a good day, but his stance was downright deadly. I didn't want to know what would happen if we were forced to fight to the death. It might be a very long, bloody battle.

Flora held his gaze for a while. Just when I thought there

might be a fight, she lowered her eyes. Without another word, she stalked off toward the house.

It took all my willpower not to ball my hands into fists and demand to know what she'd wanted Kerr to say. Instead, I turned toward the black sedan and jerked the car door open. Caitlyn stared at my outstretched hand before tentatively accepting my help.

"Everyone, go back to your duties. You'll accomplish nothing gathered around here acting mad." Only a few people began to shuffle off. When I snarled, the rest followed suit. I leveled a stare at Kerr. "My study, now!"

Wolves still dressed in their tartans littered the castle's long hallways. All of them lowered their gaze as I passed with Caitlyn. My beast was on edge after the funeral. He'd just started to calm down when we pulled up to the unruly crowd in front of the Pack's headquarters. Now he wanted to tear into something or someone, and while the idea of letting out my pent-up aggression would undoubtedly calm my wolf, I couldn't fly off the handle like that. I needed to temper my emotions and remember my father's lessons on how best to handle my wolves.

Before I met Kerr in the study, I needed to be sure Caitlyn was safe. My hand remained in hers as we walked, and I couldn't be sure whether it was to keep her from running or to keep my beast from getting too out of control. Either way, the trip to the bedroom proved uneventful, but I could feel the wolves' eyes on us.

I snapped the bedroom door shut and leaned against it, closing my eyes as I took deep breaths to calm myself. When I regained control of my beast, I opened them again and Caitlyn was standing by the foot of the bed. Her concerned gaze immediately dropped in submission, and the simple action rocked me to the core. Did she think I'd ever hurt her? My heart ached in my chest, and my brogue thickened. "Stay in the bedroom, and if ye know what's good for ye, only open the door for me, love. Aye?"

She nodded, still keeping her gaze low. "Aye." With a sigh, she briefly glanced up at me before returning to the floor. "I'm sorry things are shite right now. *Och*, I never bloody intended to cause such a mess."

My anger melted a little at her words. Truth be told, she hadn't done this all on her own. I'd played a role in it too. If I'd been able to squash Alistair's reckless behavior, maybe he wouldn't have snapped and brought her back here. Although, in that case, the downside was I never would've met her. Caitlyn aroused something in my wolf that I'd never experienced with any other woman. It wasn't often you found that kind of connection, even with a mate. I imagined a life with her that I didn't even know my wolf craved. "Hush now, love. I've got to meet with Kerr. We can discuss this after the wake." A frown curved the corners of my lips, and I pulled her into a gentle hug.

Reluctantly, I let go of her and then left the bedroom. Fewer wolves were roaming the halls now. Hopefully, they'd gone to the grand hall, where the wake would take place. My nose twitched at the faint scent of food, and my stomach rumbled. If the Pack wasn't on the brink of combusting, I might be there too.

A headache built behind my eyes as I approached the study. Kerr was waiting beside the door. The stress of the funeral combined with the shite that came afterward was piling up fast. If I didn't find time to shift, my head would explode. Though from the dark expression on Kerr's face, that might happen sooner rather than later. I closed the door behind us for privacy, and we seated ourselves. Silence stretched between us as the large man fidgeted in the chair across from me. Kerr wasn't known to act this way. He was always like a strong, unbreakable rock that I could depend on.

I cleared my throat, bringing his attention back to me. "Speak."

"Aye, m'laird. My apologies." Creases lined his forehead, and he pursed his lips before letting out a sigh. "Yer brother is coming home. After everything that's happened since Alistair brought Caitlyn here, I've had my uncertainties that ye were still fit to lead us. Yer...woman seems to take up a larger portion of yer time than yer responsibilities as Alpha. Yer father taught ye to be a leader. It's who yer meant to be." Kerr kept his gaze and his voice low. "But I haven't seen that leader for some time now. Ye should have chosen yer Pack over the lass."

"If this is about the funeral..."

"I contacted Ewan before that debacle."

If I weren't so angry, my jaw likely would've dropped to the table. My brother had wanted nothing to do with the Pack after my father died. If it had been up to me, I never would've taken over in the first place. Part of me was thrilled Ewan was returning, but as Alpha, I knew it wouldn't be a rainbow-filled family reunion. He'd have a choice in what happened next. We weren't on the best of terms, so my imagination ran rampant with images of how it would go down with snarling wolves ready to rip each other to shreds.

My jaw clenched so hard it hurt. If Ewan came back, he was probably coming to take over. Alpha wolves didn't just hand over the reins, even if part of me had yearned for that many times. We had a duty to our wolves and a tradition to fight to the death for our Packs when challenged by an aggressor. Granted, I'd wanted to kill my brother more than once when we were younger, but that was sibling rivalry and my threat was never real. I could never kill Ewan.

I had no idea how they'd convinced my runaway brother

to finally fulfill his duties to the Pack. He'd never wanted to take the reins even after our father had trained Ewan to replace him. Maybe he wanted to come back to see how much I'd faltered in our father's place. It wouldn't surprise me. Rubbing shite in my face was typical for Ewan.

Kerr's frown deepened. "I'm sorry, laird—"

"For fuck's sake." I exploded from my chair. "Dinnae call me that. Not now." Part of me wished Caitlyn were here to strengthen my resolve in what I would face when my brother came to challenge me. I needed my mate. My Pack needed a strong female leader by my side, and I wished they could see that in Caitlyn. When she wasn't putting herself at needless risk, her presence comforted me and calmed my beast and her tenacity was something our Pack could use. "When will my brother arrive?"

"He has obligations to take care of in Oslo first, but he should be here in about a week." Kerr cleared his throat again. "I hope you're able to redeem yerself in the eyes of the Pack before then." With that last snipe, he walked out and closed the door.

My legs buckled under my weight, pitching me back into my chair. The world as I knew it was crumbling beneath me. What in the bloody hell was I going to do? The majority of the Pack was against me, especially my second-in-command.

I leaned my head back against the chair and took a deep breath. If I stood any chance of undoing this and keeping myself and Caitlyn safe, I needed to rally my supporters. I doubted much could be done about whether my brother declared his rightful challenge against me, but I'd stand a better chance with a new second-in-command. Unfortunately, I trusted only one man to fulfill those shoes now, and he was in northwestern Scotland.

It was time for Colin to come home.

7

CAITLYN

he television blared the news as I paced Dougal's bedroom. Something was wrong. The tension between Dougal and Kerr had hit a breaking point, and the gathering of wolves out front had been ready to fight again when we pulled up. I could kick myself for having caused Dougal more shite. My fear and stubbornness were to blame. Again.

Perhaps if I'd put my antisocial wereleopard who refused to listen to anyone in her place, things would be different. The Pack would be calmer and focused on their loss instead of acting against their Alpha.

Shite.

Maybe I should've tried to barge into the study with Dougal and Kerr. I hadn't dared to suggest it because I'd already caused enough damage for one day. If they'd wanted me to be there, they would have invited me. My leopardess knew where she wasn't wanted, but part of her purred protectively when it came to Dougal. Besides, I doubted the meeting would be pleasant. Would Kerr convince Dougal to get rid of me? Would Dougal go along with it? What if they forced his hand?

My heart raced, and my cat was ready to claw Kerr's eyes out. I balled my hands into fists before relaxing them again. Tears welled, blurring my vision. I didn't want my relationship with Dougal to end.

The leopardess beneath my skin slammed upward. Pain ached in my hands as her claws extended from my fingertips. I stared at my hands and arms in dismay. Thick, pale yellow fur with rosettes began sprouting across my skin.

Bloody hell!

I closed my eyes and sucked in a few calming breaths. If I didn't shove down my emotions, I'd be taken over by my beast. I couldn't let that happen. Not now when things were so tense, and especially not in a household full of wolves. As my heart rate slowed, I focused on reversing the shift.

The last time I'd unintentionally shifted was when I'd been a young girl, still unaware of how to control my beast. The consequences of that shift haunted me to this day. Ever since then, I'd struggled to keep my feelings under control and not let my beast have full rein unless we were in the midst of a battle.

With the shift back to human complete, I nearly slumped onto the floor. It took way too much willpower to get my leopard to relent. Normally she was more easygoing, but neither of us were at our best.

My thoughts broke when a key rattled in the lock. Every muscle in my body tensed, especially after Dougal's earlier warning. However, I doubted he gave many people the key to his chambers. When Dougal walked in, my breath released. He'd returned, and not too long after leaving, either. Maybe things hadn't been so bad. Then the shell-shocked expression on his face melted my smile. I slowly walked toward him, still keeping my gaze low.

"Is everything okay?" My voice was barely a whisper, but he glanced over at me with a hint of resignation. "What's going on, Dougal?"

"My brother is coming home."

My heart skipped a beat, and dizziness almost knocked me off my feet. I sunk onto the bed before I'd end up collapsing.

Growing up, Colin had told me many things about werewolf society. He'd hoped to keep me informed so that I'd stay safe. If he'd only known how handy that information would become... I didn't know what I'd do without it. The one thing I'd learned from Colin is that when an Alpha male claimed leadership and another challenged them, they fought...to the death.

"When will he arrive?" My voice sounded hollow.

"He'll be here in a week." Dougal crossed the distance between us and sat beside me on the bed. He cupped the back of my neck and pressed a gentle kiss to my forehead. I wrapped my arms around him, needing his warmth, the comfort of his presence. "Kerr talked my brother into coming. He betrayed me, and said I'd chosen you over the Pack." He gritted his teeth, making the muscles in his jaw clench. "I've done so much for them. This one time I may have faltered, and this is how he repays me." He looked like he wanted to spit. "I need a strong wolf at my side right now. Someone I can count on, and who values you too. Colin needs to come home."

My heart pounded in my chest, unsure if I liked this idea. If Colin became part of this, they would both be in danger. If he didn't, Dougal would be left to fend for himself. He had backers within the Pack, the fight at the funeral had proved that, but he needed someone strong and capable. No one else here gave a shite about me. Their loyalty was to their Alpha. Colin was the only one who would care about what might happen to me if Dougal couldn't hang onto his position. The chances of Dougal coming out alive were thin if he lacked support. He needed all the bodies he could get in case the situation descended into chaos.

"I might know a few places we could look," I said, pulling back enough to lock gazes with him. "Come with me. I hate the thought of ye being here alone." My throat was raw with emotion and unshed tears. "I dinnae want anything to happen to ye. I wouldn't be able to handle it."

He gave me a crooked grin, but it didn't reach all the way to his eyes. "I'll be fine, love. My only danger shall be heartache from missing you."

I couldn't help but smile even as I smacked him on the chest. "Stay safe for me. Please?" My voice cracked a little, and I cleared my throat.

Dougal pulled me into a hug, squeezing me as if he didn't want to let go. "Aye, love. Dinnae worry. Nothing will happen. Not unless one of my Pack members challenge me, but they will wait patiently for my brother to do the honors." A grimace tightened his lips, and he shook his head. "How could they want Ewan over me? My brother abandoned his responsibilities. He left the Pack. Can't they see that? After my father died, he ran away to join a Pack in Norway. Now they're expecting him to be the leader they've always wanted? Someone who could replace my father? Unbelievable."

I nuzzled my face against his chest, my leopardess fearing for her mate. "I hope they dinnae come to learn their lesson. What's the chance of him actually coming back?" Thin strands of hope weaved their way around my heart, even though I shouldn't let them. "He could get cold feet again and stay in Norway."

The grim look on Dougal's face confirmed my mistake. "There's a chance of that, but I know how he is. He'll likely come, if nothing else to rub it in my face." He leaned his head against the top of mine. "We were never close growing up. He always preferred tearing me down and teasing me rather than being my brother, someone I could lean on. What hurts worst isn't that he left me to handle the Pack's leadership, but the fact he left me when I needed support after our father died. My father and I were close, even with all of his duties. He always made time for me...for both of us, even if he was busy. Life has been hard with him gone." He buried his face into my hair, drawing in a shaky breath. "I wouldn't put it past the arsehole to come all this way to strike at me again. To issue a challenge for a Pack he doesn't give a shite about."

My heart ached, and I held Dougal tighter, not wanting to ever let go. "I'm here for ye. You're not alone anymore. Ye never have to be alone again."

"Thanks, love," he said. "I know that you're here for me."

While Colin and I had our own issues, we'd never treated each other cruelly. We strove to support one another, in our own kind of way. When it truly mattered, Colin had my back, just like when I'd dropped everything to try to rescue him. Was he okay? He hadn't gotten in touch, and I'd tried ringing his mobile. The blasted thing kept going to his voicemail. When he was here, he'd been barely recognizable as the brother I'd known before his capture. More like a wounded animal. I only hoped Colin and the people around him were safe.

Dougal and I remained in each other's arms, holding one another for several minutes. The thought of leaving him sickened my stomach. Realizing I'd tried to walk away from him before didn't help my sour belly. I'd been so stupid to think life without him would be better. At least his wolf hadn't let me go through with that mistake. Being dragged back wasn't fun, but I hadn't struggled much because I didn't want a repeat visit to the cage. I'd learned how unpleasant it was with Alistair.

Dougal broke the moment and leaned back, putting me at arm's length. "I could stay here with you forever. Sadly, I have to attend the wake, and you should get on the road sooner than later." He caressed my cheek, and I leaned into his touch. "It'll be okay, love. You'll be back in no time." He opened his sporran and handed me the key to his Jeep, along with a few hundred quid.

This all felt so final, as if I'd never see him again. "What if...?" I couldn't even finish the thought because my mind was spinning from all the horrible ways this could end.

He lifted my chin so that I met his eyes. "Hush, love. Dinnae fash yerself. I'll be fine." He wrapped an arm around me, gently tugging me closer, and pressed a kiss against my lips. "Take care when you find Colin. I told you before that I'd spoken with him and ensured he wasn't a danger. But I don't know if that's entirely true. I had to weigh the threat to himself versus the danger he'd be to you and the Pack. He traveled to the village of Durness."

My heart raced at Dougal's words. "Wait, what? How could ye have allowed Colin to leave if he wasn't in his best frame of mind?" I pulled away from his touch and shook my head, unable to believe what I was hearing. "You should've told me where he was. If anything's happened to him—"

"I'm sorry. Perhaps I should've told you, but I'd promised him I would look after you. If you'd known, you would've gone after him, and the lad needed his space to heal." He brushed his thumb over my cheek, then leaned in to kiss the top of my head. "If you need anything, ring me immediately. A couple other wolves I know live up that way. I can have them assist ye if you need it."

I opened my mouth to protest more, but the tender kiss on my head stole away those words. His primary goal was keeping me and his Pack safe. He had the best of intentions, so I couldn't fault him. He had to focus on the Pack as a whole, not individuals. Besides, he didn't get much credit for the good he'd done by those around him. I refused to cast more blame upon him.

After a few moments, I nodded. "He's in Durness? It makes sense he'd go there. Mum took us to the sleepy village on holiday when we were children." I took a deep breath, then slowly let it out. "We hated it at the time. It was peaceful and isolated. Not exactly the ideal trip for two young kids. Then again, it was what we needed. Colin was starting to show signs of being a werewolf, and my control over my leopard was lacking. No one was there to teach me how to cope. I dinnae find someone to help me until later when I discovered the Pard shortly after Colin became involved with the Pack." I shook away the memories and looked up into Dougal's beautiful blue eyes. "Are ye sure you're going to be okay?"

"You never cease to amaze me, love. You're brave. I don't know how anyone could manage without support at a young age like that." Dougal smiled, and it faintly touched his eyes. "Aye, love. Take care of yourself on the trip. I love you."

My voice broke a little. "I love you too."

Few wolves were around as we walked out to the side of the castle where the Jeep was parked. There was lots of talking and some laughter coming from the direction of the grand hall, so I presumed the Pack was at the wake, reminiscing about their two deceased wolves.

"Drive safely," Dougal said, then gave me one last kiss. He closed the door and took a step back.

Heaviness burdened my heart as I pulled away. I took one last glimpse of him in the rearview mirror before I fixed my gaze on the long gravel driveway in front of me.

8

DOUGAL

*W*atching Caitlyn start her journey down the driveway broke my heart a little. Talking with her about my brother wasn't easy, but I'd tried my hardest to stay strong despite the emotions squeezing at my chest. She never ceased to amaze me, either. Finding out she'd been on her own with no one to guide her in controlling her beast saddened me. I'd grown up knowing about my abilities and learning how to use them. How would I have turned out if I'd been in Caitlyn's shoes? Maybe I should be more patient with her. It certainly explained her wild, stubborn streak that attracted my wolf.

I turned at the top of the stairs to track the Jeep until it turned out of sight. Why had I thought sending her into the Highlands alone to fetch her brother was a good idea again?

I shoved my fingers through my hair as I walked inside to attend the wake. If I'd gone with her, I'd know she was safe, but I had responsibilities to the Pack. Then again, I also had a duty to her as my mate. The two priorities seemed to oppose one another constantly instead of simply coexisting, but any relationship was a delicate balance.

The wake was still in full swing when I walked into the grand hall. A few wolves gave me steely glares, but once they saw Caitlyn wasn't with me, everyone relaxed again. Whatever they might think, this event was neither the time nor place for more brawling. Especially not when the aroma of quality Scotch and good food was teasing my nostrils.

Mairi had done her best to make this a special gathering to honor the departed wolves.

Kerr sat in his chair near the head of the table, drinking and talking merrily with a few of the lads around him. His boisterous laughter rang through the room, and he slapped the man beside him on the back.

Mairi stepped up beside me as I walked toward the laird's chair. "Laird, I'm happy you're here. I was becoming a wee bit nervous that you might not show. Where's your mate?" She glanced toward the hallway as if Caitlyn would appear. "Isn't she coming?"

"Nae, she's not. After earlier, I'm sure that's for the best too, aye?" Should I mention that Caitlyn wasn't even here right now? Out on the road, she might be safer. The Scottish Highlands weren't small, so the threat of a rogue wolf finding her was slim. Besides, Mairi was a good, loyal wolf. "She's away from the castle."

"She is? I see." Curiosity sparked in Mairi's eyes. "But, aye, I suspect you're right." She beamed at me with what almost looked like pride. "The lass sure can fight. The way she pounced on grumpy old Tamhas was a true sight."

"It was a sight all right. Nearly gave me a heart attack. If anything happened to her, I'd be beside myself." I shook my head and moved with her out of earshot from the rest of the wolves. Having any semblance of privacy within the grand hall was nigh impossible with the Pack around, but I didn't need to make my words easily overheard. "I wish there wasn't a clash between her and the Pack. If they could see the side of her I knew, they would know she's a good lass regardless of her species." I ran my hand through my hair again.

Mairi placed her small hand on my arm. "Laird, if I may be blunt, she's partly done it to herself by remaining so isolated. No one has gotten the chance to get to know her." She shrugged a dainty shoulder. "Not that I'm saying it's the lass's fault. This must be a challenge for her, but it's just my wee observation."

I nodded, feeling a migraine form behind my eyes. "That's true. *Och*, I've tried talking with her about it. She's not fond of werewolves. Some have shown her nothing but cruelty in the past for being a feline shifter."

"The poor lass. I cannae begin to understand why someone would treat another being like that." Mairi glanced toward the Pack engaged in conversation at the table. "Have a seat, laird. I'll be there in less than a minute." She gave me another bright smile before darting off toward the kitchen.

Kerr was staring in my direction when I looked toward the end of the table. He tilted his head toward me in respect, but he appeared uneasy. At least he didn't excuse himself and leave. Even if he'd betrayed me by convincing my brother to retake the Pack, I wouldn't stoop to acting out during the wake.

The other wolves seated near the head of the table cooled their laughter and merriment for a moment when I sat down. We sat there and stared at one another. Within moments, Mairi brought me food and a drink, just as she'd said.

Kerr rose to his feet and lifted his glass in the air. The room fell silent. "To our friends, brothers, and Pack mates who are no longer with us. Anyone who knew Duncan knew he was usually soft-spoken and disliked conflict. He had a rocky start in life, but he found a family with us. The lad will be sorely missed. He left us far too soon. And Alistair… That crabby bastard was known for being a troublemaker, but he was also someone who stood up for what he believed in. You could always throw back a few pints and talk with him at the end of a rough day. Let them both rest peacefully. *Slàinte!"*

"Well said, Kerr." I nodded to him as he retook his seat.

"Cheers. They should be remembered fondly despite any shortcomings," Kerr said.

Kerr wasn't talking about Duncan. The big man had greatly respected him, and his death hit Kerr hard. Alistair hadn't been a bad guy until he found Caitlyn in Colin's home. But he hadn't been a jovial, friendly guy either. Like Kerr had said, he'd been a crabby, troublemaking bastard most of the time.

"That they should." I continued to eat and converse with the wolves near me, including Kerr. We joked about the good times with the deceased and discussed the memories they left behind. When I'd walked into the room, I hadn't been sure how my presence would be taken here. Not after what happened in the study with Kerr's news. This felt like I was with family and friends, not people who would rather see me dead because they didn't like who I'd chosen as a mate. However, the migraine didn't leave me.

My beast gnashed his teeth, ready to run free. I'd kept myself on a tight leash for a while, with barely a chance to shift, aside from killing Alistair. If I didn't give in to my wolf, it might be harder to handle him when I needed to remain in control. I didn't want to leave myself vulnerable to losing my temper and causing more potential harm to those I cared for.

When enough time had passed, I excused myself from the group I'd been chatting with. My first thought was to go to my bedroom, but nothing and no one waited for me there. My heart ached again, remembering Caitlyn's absence. The beast's desire to run free led me out the front door. I drew in the crisp scent of fresh air mixed with Scots pine and a variety of plant types from the castle's lavish gardens.

With a quick glance to make sure I was alone, I let out a deep breath and took off toward the trees surrounding the property. Once there, I shed my clothing.

Completely naked, I knelt in the grass and welcomed the wolf, allowing him to take over my body. The beast stretched out from within me. Claws poked through the tips of my fingers, and tendons all over my body snapped and bones broke before twisting into my wolf's form. A tail stretched from my spine, and fur rippled out of my skin almost in a wave. When the painful transformation was complete, we let out a huff, then took a long, lazy stretch. We ran through the pine trees as fast as we could, my beast's instincts guiding our steps.

He wasn't pleased with my decision to let Caitlyn travel to Durness by herself either, but what else could I have done? Allow the Pack to believe I was choosing Caitlyn over them? Alphas weren't tied to their headquarters. It wasn't uncommon for a laird to take trips, but with the ever-growing tension, traveling would do more harm than good right now.

Our nostrils twitched as the woodland scent of a hare sparked our interest. We slowed a little, not wanting to scare off our prey. We stalked forward, stepping lightly through the trees to avoid drawing attention. The last time we'd run free in this form had been with the Pack during the full moon. That had been several days ago. If the wolf didn't get out and stretch his legs, he tended to get cranky. It was even worse when we were dealing with this mountain of stress. It was a wonder I hadn't already snapped and ended up like Colin.

But no... Comparing what I was going through to what he'd endured was unthinkable. The lad had been through more shite than anyone should have to bear in a lifetime, let alone in less than a year. I wouldn't want to put my worst enemy through what he'd experienced.

If I didn't quiet my thoughts, I'd ruin this. Shaking our head, I forced myself to shut up and continue focusing on the hare.

The beast didn't care for my internal monologue either. He snatched control, and we crept forward, moving quietly and carefully toward our prey as to not snap any fallen tree branches or alert the animal in any way.

The brown hare perked his little head up and twisted his ears around like antennas. Our heart picked up at the thought he might take off, and we'd have a real hunt. Instead, the rabbit leaned back down and nibbled on some vegetation again. He seemed oblivious to our presence. No chase, no thrill.

We sat on our haunches, staring at the wee animal. The beast wasn't in the mood for an easy kill. We wanted more than this—something to challenge our skill and get our blood pumping. This would be merely slaughtering a hare.

After the delightful meal Mairi cooked, we weren't incredibly hungry. Of course, the desire for meat and the taste of coppery blood rushing down our throat interested us, but it didn't provide much incentive at the moment.

We lay down in the grass nearby, calmly watching the rabbit as he continued munching. Huffing a breath, we rested our head on our paws. What else did I have to do now that Caitlyn was gone? The Pack wouldn't need much tonight. Probably nothing significant would happen until my brother arrived. I'd just have to bide my time and keep my cool. The hare's ears twisted around suddenly at the screeching of an eagle, and it darted away through the trees. We leapt to our feet, but it was soon out of sight.

It was just as well that the rabbit fled. We turned and

jogged back to where my clothes were still laid out. I sniffed around the site to be sure no one had come around while I was gone. It was clear.

The change back to my human form took more effort and force of will. It hurt like hell since I hadn't been in my wolf shape for long, and we hadn't feasted to recharge the strength the initial shift took from us.

I checked my phone before getting dressed again. No new text messages.

Part of me was relieved. I'd promised Caitlyn that she could text me if she needed to, and I'd get back to her immediately. If anything happened to her while I wasn't near my mobile, I'd be furious with myself.

The other half of me was a little sad at not hearing from her. I missed her more than I'd imagined, but she was on a mission that might be more important than I cared to admit. While I doubted she'd find much trouble on the road, I couldn't shake the uneasiness weighing heavily on me.

9

CAITLYN

$\mathcal{T}$he five-and-a-half-hour drive—not counting a small stop for a snack and the loo—had been more tiring than I'd expected, and I breathed a sigh of relief when I spotted the white sign welcoming me to Durness. I'd made a few more attempts to reach Colin's mobile on the trip, but the calls kept going straight to voicemail. Panic gripped me by the throat. If only he'd answer his damn phone. Had something happened to him? Had he hurt himself or someone else? Would I even find him alive?

I couldn't let those thoughts take over. Colin was likely relaxing along the beach, being antisocial. But each time I called without him answering made me more and more worried. Bloody hell. I'd locate him soon enough, though. Durness was a small village. Even if I had to go door-to-door asking after him, I would.

The local pub appeared up ahead, and my stomach grumbled loudly. My leopard had already begun her protest at the lack of food during the long car trip. I pulled into the parking lot for a quick bite. I'd only relented to one stop, mainly to use the loo, because my priority was to get here as fast as possible. Maybe that hadn't been the best choice for keeping my beast satisfied, but I'd rectify the situation now.

The village seemed even smaller and quainter than when we'd visited as kids, but that tended to be the way of things. I walked into the pub, which was fairly packed with people drinking and having supper. This seemed to be the happening place in town. Maybe Colin had stopped in for a drink or some food and the grey-haired, smiling bartender would know where I could begin my search.

"Come on in and have a seat, lass," the bartender said, setting a menu on the bar in front of an empty stool.

I returned his smile, trying my best to make it genuine, as I perched onto the stool. My mind raced: thoughts of my brother being in danger kept spinning through my head. But I was worried about Dougal, too. The sooner I found Colin, the sooner we could head back to Edinburgh. I covered my mouth as I yawned. Maybe I needed some rest first, if I'd be successful in finding him.

The menu had several traditional Scottish dishes, as well as the usual pub food. It all looked so good. My tummy grumbled again.

"It's not often we see a new face in town," the bartender said, leaning against the bar. "Though we've been getting some new visitors lately. Must be tourist season."

My heart beat a little faster, but I tried to appear relaxed. "I guess it is. Ye wouldn't happen to know where I might find this lad, would ye?" I'd kept the only picture I had of me and Colin in my wallet since his abduction, and I pulled it out now to show the bartender.

The cheerful-looking man stroked his chin, as if he needed to think about it. "Who wants to know?"

My shoulders tensed, and anger washed over me. Why would he hold back answers? My beast rumbled her displeasure. Only when the bartender's eyes widened did I realize she'd made the sound out loud. "Sorry, I'm hungrier than I initially thought, I guess. I'm his sister, and I really need to find him."

"The name's Mike Melville." He tilted his head toward me. "If you satisfy that hunger, I might remember where your brother could be staying."

My eyebrows lifted at his statement. He'd only tell me if I bought something. "I'm Caitlyn." I scanned the menu one more time. Even though I was famished, I shouldn't order too much food. A petite woman like me eating so much could draw suspicion. "I'll have the steak pie and chips." He nodded but remained in place, as if implying I wasn't finished. "A Scotch ale too." I rarely imbibed, but after the long day I'd had, I craved something to help me relax, even if my fast metabolism made alcohol fairly moot. I could still get drunk if I really overdid it, but it took a lot of effort.

"Right away, lass." Mike winked at me before heading toward the kitchen.

I checked my phone again. It'd be pointless to try calling anyone in this place. The drum of conversation was loud enough that you needed to pay close attention to hear the person you were speaking with. Strangely enough—or not—I missed Dougal more than I'd thought I would. His presence would've made the trip more fun, but he needed to attend the wake and prove to his Pack they were wrong about him. I texted Dougal, telling him I'd arrived in Durness. I may have also sent a kissy-face emoji. My heart warmed when he immediately sent me one back and said he was glad I'd made it safely.

Mike placed the ale in front of me. "So, you're the lad's sister, aye?"

The way he said that made me wonder, but I nodded. The ale tasted better than I'd thought it would.

"Ye came a long way to find him then, I presume."

Apparently, Mike enjoyed talking in circles. What had Colin told the bartender about himself? My brother didn't open up to people easily, so this conversation concerned me.

"I did. Will you tell me where he's staying, or not?" It took all of my self-control to keep my tone pleasant when all I wanted was to climb over this bar and strangle the bartender.

"Ah, there's the temperament. Ye are related to him." He grabbed a pad of paper and a pen from behind the bar and scratched out an address on it. Before I could take a peek, he folded the paper and set it on his side of the bar. If I stretched over the bar top, I could grab for it, but he might tear it up. "You can have this when you're finished eating. Just be careful. Yer brother is going through some things with some not-so-nice people."

My eyes widened, and the chest-clenching fear I'd experienced before came rushing back. A bell rang, and Mike walked away before I could ask what he meant. I should've gone looking for him sooner.

A twinge of anger hit me. Dougal had only done what he thought was right, but he should have told me he'd known where my brother was all along. Maybe I could've visited him and I'd have known how much Colin needed my help. I'd never forgive myself if something terrible happened to Colin.

Dougal shouldn't have let him go off on his own. What if Colin had attacked someone, or killed them? Or worse, what if he'd changed them into a werewolf?

My throat closed up, and I pushed the ale aside. My nerves rebelled at the thought of food, even though my beast still wanted to dig her teeth into some steak.

Mike waltzed back over with my plate and set it before me. "Don't look so worried, lass. It'll be all right. Colin's capable of handling himself."

I nodded and kept my gaze on the scrap of paper as I ate.

Each bite brought me closer to seeing Colin again. My leopard nearly purred with satisfaction at getting food in my stomach. I reached for more chips, but when I glanced down, I blinked in surprise at my empty plate.

The bartender stood at the other end of the bar, chatting with a few people who I could only assume were some of his regulars. I stretched over the counter, grabbed the piece of paper, and dropped enough money to cover the bill. He could keep the change. I just wanted to find Colin. He glanced over at me and started in my direction, but I was gone before he could reach me.

I hopped in Dougal's Jeep and put the address into the GPS.

Colin's place was a decent clip from town, but I made good time. No vehicles were parked outside the cottage when I arrived, so I parked a little way off. If Colin was in trouble, I should investigate the area instead of waltzing into danger. My nose might not be up to werewolf standards, but I sure as shite could take care of myself. I sniffed around, keeping my distance from anything that might momentarily capture my scent.

Mike had said Colin was dealing with unpleasant people, but there was no telling whether they were ordinary human men or werewolves. Humans didn't alarm me, but my body still ached from Alistair's beatdown.

Memories of him encroached on my thoughts, and I balled my hands into fists while taking deep breaths to calm myself. The cool, fresh air, with its hint of the sea, helped bring me peace. Alistair was dead. I'd seen him buried. Would he always hold this kind of power over me?

When I'd completed my search of the land around the cottage, I pulled into the driveway and hopped out to look around some more. My leopard wanted me to shed my human skin and run free, but now wasn't the best time for that. We needed to wait for Colin to hurry his arse home. The crunch of footsteps on the gravel driveway stirred my attention.

Colin stood there, staring at Dougal's Jeep with confusion. He scanned the area and stalked toward the cottage. When I tapped his shoulder, he whirled on me, his hand jerking toward my throat.

With a grin, I leapt away from him, but pain ached through my side at the sharp movement, making me wince. "Aye, ye haven't changed much. So tense." A frown curved my lips. "Nae, something's happened. What's wrong, Colin?" Did this have to do with those people Mike talked about?

Colin sighed, then raked a hand through his hair. "What the bloody hell are ye doin' here, Caitlyn?"

I'd driven way too far to deal with any shite from him. "I asked first." Frustration built within my chest, and I crossed my arms.

He turned away from me and scanned the area again, then balled his hands into fists. "It's a long story. You shouldn't have come all this way. When a man goes off, he expects some privacy." Despite his words, his anger seemed to have dampened a little. He rarely stayed upset with me for long. Neither of us could. We were family, after all.

"Aye, but the typical brother doesn't leave his unconscious sister in the care of a Pack of unfamiliar werewolves." I lifted an eyebrow at him, still feeling the sting from that.

A low rumbling growl built in his chest, and he ran his hand through his hair again. Conflicting emotions slid across his face as he shook his head. "You were fine. We both know that. Now, what are you doing here?"

That was a good enough answer, for now. I doubted I'd get much more from him even if I kept pushing. But how was I supposed to tell him the Scottish Pack was falling apart, and Dougal was in trouble? Biting my lower lip, I focused on the dull pain from Alistair's punch before responding. "I know ye went away because of what happened. I've been worried about you, but...there's some trouble at home in Edinburgh. Dougal sent me for you since, while you're not his favorite person, you care about me and the Pack." Maybe I shouldn't have said that about him not being Dougal's favorite person. Shite.

Colin cocked his head to one side, his expression puzzled. "Why didn't you call?"

How could he ask that? I narrowed my eyes at him and frowned. "As ye darn well should know. I tried calling several times over the span of the last few days, but you never answered." This wasn't exactly the reunion I'd planned, but at least Colin appeared safe. I chewed on my lower lip again.

Colin watched the gesture with a strange sadness that made me stop. For a moment, he seemed to drift off to somewhere else, but then he blinked, breaking the spell. "Right. I'm sorry. I should've checked my mobile." He met my gaze. "How did you find me?"

My smile didn't reach my eyes. "Dougal told me, and I remembered that we visited here on holiday once with Mum. It made sense you'd come here to get away." I looked toward the cottage, then back at him. "The bartender in town said you were around these parts. I let my nose do the rest. While I'm not quite as good a tracker as some werewolves, I'm not horrible." That was only a partial truth, since the bartender had given me his address, but I didn't think the truth would make him feel any better.

His face reddened, and he looked like he wanted to spit in frustration. But he shook off the emotion after a moment. "Well, I'm glad you found me. I need to start packing then."

It surprised me he was so on board to leave. Maybe the trip had helped him work through whatever he'd needed to do. Or perhaps he needed to escape from the people he'd gotten in trouble with. "Yes, you do. We're heading out first thing in the morning." Regardless of the reason, at least I had my brother back. I patted his shoulder and started walking up the path to the cottage.

Colin trailed after me, and the closer I got to the house, the more anxiety I felt from him. What was he trying to hide? He unlocked the door, and I glanced around at the place. It looked quaint and decent. Nothing out of the... My nose wrinkled.

"Nice. If only it didn't smell so heavily of booze and..." I turned to face Colin and raised an eyebrow. "Sex?" I'd been through hell, and he was living it up. "Some lovely local girl?"

I could only imagine the shite he'd been up to.

"N—" His voice broke, and he shook his head. Pain etched his face, and he cleared his throat before trying again. "A lass on holiday. That's all." Even though he tried to sound casual, his emotions made his voice take on a hard edge. I'd never seen him like this before. He'd never shown his feelings for other lasses he'd been in relationships with, but I now could tell he was hiding something. This lass must've meant something to him, especially for him to let himself get close after what he'd been through. He turned away from me and started packing up his things.

"Sounds like an adventure. We...uh." I cleared my throat and slumped onto the couch. "We buried yer father. We dinnae ken when you'd be getting back, so... Aye. It was nice enough, and the Pack was there, minus a few oddballs." I leaned my head forward, staring at the carpet in front of me. How could I tell him about the utter mess happening within the Pack? A mess I'd caused by being in his Alpha's life and going to his father's funeral. I clenched my hands on my knees. "I thought you'd want to know before we got back."

Rising anger oozed from Colin, but he stomped it down. "Thank you," he said, emotion roughening his voice again.

I glanced up at him and gave him a small smile. It was all I could muster. "No worries, mate. Been through worse than a funeral."

"Aye. Guess you have. Well, I'll get the rest of my things packed. Have ye eaten?" His brogue thickened a little. "I could fix us something."

"Dinnae fash about cooking. I can do it." I bounced up from the couch. Even though I'd had a bite at the pub, my leopard was still starving. "Just go on and pack." Once he got everything together, we could sleep and be ready bright and early in the morning for our trip home.

"Thanks." He headed off toward the bedroom, probably doing a walk-through of the place, making sure everything was tidy and in order.

I gathered the few supplies from his fridge and pantry to get busy cooking. My leopard wanted to be free and hunt something to eat, but this would be better than nothing. A knock on the door distracted me from my thoughts, and I froze in front of the stove. Could that be the troublemakers the bartender had warned about? I glanced at Colin, who had just stopped in the kitchen and frowned. "Expecting anyone?"

"No, I'm not." Something like hope flickered across his face before he shut it down. "Stay back. I'll take a look to see who it is."

I glared but shot him a questioning frown. "I may not be fully healed, but I'm not a weakling, Colin. Don't ye even think of me as such."

He shook his head. "Nae, I wouldn't do ye that disservice after all you've done for me, sis. Hang back a little."

I turned off the stove, then brushed past him on my way toward the bedroom. Pain radiated through my still-tender side, and I instantly regretted bumping into him. I worked to keep the pain out of my voice. "Fine. But if I hear anything confrontational, I'm not going to have you standing alone."

"All right."

The bedroom smelled strongly of sex. The sheets were disheveled, and it appeared to be the least tidy room. My appetite soured a little at being in there. I considered removing the sheets so I could sit on the bed, but I settled for pacing back and forth like the caged leopard within me. I could faintly hear my brother talking to a woman. The doors and walls were thicker than I would've expected.

I clenched my hands into fists and wondered what things were like for Dougal back in Edinburgh. Was he okay? My heart ached at the thought of what was to come. I worried about his brother challenging him... What if I didn't make it back in time?

An authoritative male voice came through and startled me. "Do you want to let us in, werewolf?"

Why the hell would anyone know Colin was a werewolf here? Why would he have told someone, unless it was another shifter? Dougal mentioned there were other werewolves here, though.

I closed my eyes and took a deep breath, regretting it as I got a nose full of sex. I pushed the scent aside and cracked the door to search out the two newcomers. They smelled like nothing I'd ever experienced before. Aquatic and otherworldly. That was saying a lot coming from a wereleopard. It took all of my willpower to stay in the bedroom. I wanted to march out there and figure out the meaning of this, but I wanted to respect Colin's space.

Silently, I closed the door again, but I couldn't stop myself from eavesdropping. I sat on the floor with my back against the door. As the conversation continued, I could tell this had to be related to the woman Colin fucked. He actually sounded happier than I'd heard him in a while. They talked for a long time. Apparently, the older man was the girl's father, and there was mention of a pelt, so maybe she was a seal shifter. The only thing that fit the description were selkies, but they were creatures of myths and legends, right?

"With this, you will be her human husband, caretaker of her, lover of her. If I find out that you've harmed a hair on her head, you are as good as dead."

I leapt to my feet, lightly smacking my head against the doorknob. No one would hurt my brother. Although the father calling Colin her human husband amused me way too much. Should it? What exactly happened once he left the Pack? I doubted Colin would hurt the girl, especially since he seemed to care for her, but he was far from human. Far from safe.

"I swear not to hurt her. We will be leaving first thing in the morning, though. We need to visit Edinburgh on important business."

Bloody wanker! Just spill all of our plans.

And to take some girl with us on a mission as dangerous as ours? I couldn't believe it. He hadn't even asked for my opinion! He got all weak in the knees over some lass. My hand hovered over the doorknob. I wanted to give my input and tell them it was a terrible idea for her to go along, but the troubled emotions he'd shown when I mentioned the sex held me back. This lass—whoever she was—really meant something to him.

The bedroom still had things to be packed, and I grabbed stuff Colin had left lying around and shoved it into his bag. If I had to be stuck in here, I might as well finish getting the room in order. When I was done, I dropped his bag on the floor at the foot of the bed. At this point, I didn't care who knew I was here. My leopard was hungry and feeling way too caged. If I didn't get out of this room soon, I might chew into someone.

"Come on out, sis." Colin's voice sent relief through me and a tinge of panic. I'd actually be meeting whoever was out there. The woman who had captured Colin's heart, and her overbearing father. I didn't do well with overbearing.

I opened the door.

"I didn't know you had anyone else with you," the lass said. "You were alone earlier, when we were..." The surprised look on the blonde lass's face turned into a frown.

Colin nodded, then turned to me as I walked into the room.

I raised an eyebrow at him. Great. "Hello. Looks like ye've been busy since I last saw ye." I shoved my hands into my pockets, and amusement curved my lips, but I couldn't help staring at the innocent-looking lass. How could she possibly hold her own against werewolves? I forced a friendly smile onto my lips, but I doubted it reached my eyes.

"Yes, she came from Edinburgh to get me because she was concerned about me." Colin looked at me again, and I nodded slightly. We were pretty good at discreet glances. They'd worked well on our mother, after all.

"Right. But it's time to come home. Everyone misses you. So, we'll be heading off in my...uh...boyfriend's car tomorrow." Tension stiffened my spine, and I rolled my shoulders a little, trying to ease some of the pressure.

"A road trip? That sounds like fun." The lass's frown disappeared into a brilliant smile, and she flashed it to her father. "It'll be okay, Dad. I promise."

The father didn't look as confident as the lass. "Don't make promises you can't keep." Aye, I didn't believe it would be all right myself, and I turned into a wereleopard. How in the world would we help Dougal and protect this naïve girl? I did my best to remain still and not shuffle my feet. "But if you need anything at all, you let Ailsa know. If you want to come home early, we can make that happen." The father glared at Colin when he said that part.

Colin grimaced. His face reddened a little, but he kept his cool. "If she wants to leave me, I wouldn't stop her. I care enough about her to make sure she gets what she wants, regardless of how I feel about it." He glanced over at the stove where our food was getting cold. "Sorry, but we still have things to do before the trip tomorrow. Caitlyn was cooking supper, if you want to join us."

The blonde lass's father shook his head. "No, I'll leave you to it." He turned to his daughter. "Goodbye, my daughter." They spoke in a strangely melodic language, the likes of which I'd never heard before, and then he walked to the door. Tears slid down the lass's cheeks, but she brushed them away.

There were way too many emotions in play here. "I'll finish up dinner, Colin." I patted his shoulder, then headed for the adjoining kitchen to see what kind of mess I had to work with now. The living room and kitchen had a couple of pillars between them that blocked line-of-sight a little, but any privacy would be nil.

"Are you sure about this?" Colin asked.

"Yes. I am. I knew it was what I wanted when we talked before, and I...I guess I'm just scared."

That made two of us then.

"It'll work out, lass. I know it will." I wished I had Colin's certainty, but I really didn't. "Where are your things?" he asked.

I glanced over my shoulder to steal a peek at them. The lass had nothing with her.

She chewed on her lower lip and lowered her gaze. "I...I don't have anything."

My heart ached for her. How could someone have

nothing like that? It wasn't right. It reminded me too much of what growing up with Colin was like. Maybe that's what held his attraction, some shared history too similar to our own.

I stalked toward the living room entrance and leaned against a pillar. "I can take her shopping, if she'd like." Colin glanced over at me with relief in his gaze. "Food's ready."

The lass looked between me and Colin. "That would be very kind of you." She pulled back from Colin. "Hi, I'm Unna."

I walked toward them and held out my hand. "Hello, Unna. I'm Caitlyn." With a nod to Unna, I turned back to the kitchen. My stomach grumbled a little. We'd all need to keep our energy up if we wanted to be useful.

"Our future might not be easy," Colin said. "There's trouble among the Pack Caitlyn is with now. Trouble I walked away from before I came here. I'll do my best to protect you, but we're diving into more danger, not running from it. I don't want you to expect things to be less dangerous than they are."

At least he wasn't sugar-coating this trip. I grabbed the plates and set them on the table as Unna kissed Colin.

"I know that if I'm with you, danger is the least of my concerns. You saved my future and my life here. I don't know how I can even begin to repay you," Unna said.

If it were anyone else, I'd have been sure that comment was sexually suggestive, but from the innocence in Unna's eyes, I could tell the words came from a pure place. Bloody hell. How would the lass fare amongst a Pack of angry werewolves?

"Be with me and love me." Colin returned her kiss, deepening the gesture. The musky scent of his arousal hit my nose, and I felt like a complete voyeur.

So. Bloody. Awkward. I couldn't take much more of this. I cleared my throat loudly, hoping to grab their attention.

"Let's eat, then we can...get some sleep." Colin grinned at Unna and winked.

I just about slapped myself on the forehead. For fuck's sake. Being around them was like hanging out with two horny teenagers.

Unna's eyes widened, and a lusty grin curved her lips. "I'd like that very much."

"Well, ye two lovebirds will need to wait. The food is going to get cold if you keep kissing," I said, unable to help myself. Maybe I'd sleep in Dougal's Jeep, so I couldn't hear them have sex. I'd be fine if it weren't my fucking brother. A grimace tightened my lips, but I wiped the look off my face when they came into the kitchen. I sat in one of the chairs and focused solely on my food as we ate. The lovebirds were too busy staring at one another and giving little caresses, unable to notice how uncomfortable it was making me. When we finished eating, I offered to wash the dishes. Maybe I'd half-hoped for help, but they readily accepted my offer and made a quick retreat to the bedroom. The sink sprayed water on full blast, and I hummed a song while I did the dishes. Though, the walls didn't block as much as I'd have liked.

I hopped on the couch, trying to make this work, even if they'd forgotten to give me a pillow or a blanket, and I damn well didn't want to interrupt to ask for one considering whatever they might be doing in the bedroom. One of the decorative pillows from the couch would have to do. I pressed it over my head, but I tossed and turned as they moaned. Finally, I marched to the hallway and threw the pillow at Colin's door. There were a few giggles, and I spun on my heel for the Jeep.

Fuck this shite.

I needed rest if I was going to be awake for the *early* morning car trip. Pulling out my phone, I saw Dougal's kissy-face emoji again. I couldn't help worrying about him. Was he safe? My stomach tied itself into knots. I took a deep breath and thought of being in Dougal's arms again. Would that even happen if his brother showed up before I got back?

CAITLYN

apping on the window made me jump upright in the seat. I flailed and nearly smacked my head against the steering wheel. Colin grinned at me. My glare melted the happiness in his eyes, and I unlocked the door and stepped outside the car. "Morning."

"G'morning. Ye didn't have to sleep in the car, sis." He patted my shoulder with his free hand; the other one held one of his bags. I guessed he'd come to pack the car while Unna was washing up. "We were about to settle down when you threw the pillow at the door."

"Good to know, I guess." I hit the button on the key fob to open the trunk for his bags. The cool breeze nipped at my skin, and I rubbed my hands over my arms to keep warm. My jacket had been my pillow, and it had flown into the back seat during my jolt. "Is yer lass almost ready?" I opened the back door and grabbed the jacket, then lifted the seat.

"I am." Unna skipped down the cottage's steps with Colin's other bag. It seemed to have a strange box-like shape stretching the fabric a bit now, presumably her pelt. The thought of burying my face into my jacket and screaming was tempting, but I forced a smile. This road trip would be something else. I could already tell.

"Great. Uh, let's get on the road." I cleared my throat and hopped in the driver's seat, shutting the door before either of them could say anything else.

Colin took the bag Unna was carrying and placed it in the trunk, then he climbed into the passenger seat. The chances of them both sitting in the back were slim, but for a moment, I'd had hope. Granted, they might have made out again, and that would be awkward. Unna hopped in the seat behind Colin, and we were set to go.

Lovely Highland scenery passed by as I drove, and we kept up a light discussion for a while. But the looks Colin kept throwing my way added to my nerves, like he wanted me to get on with it and tell him what was going on. Should I with Unna in the car? It seemed strange to hold back now that she was a part of this.

I squeezed my hands on the steering wheel, my knuckles going white...he had to know about the struggle going on. "Och, I guess ye want to ken what's happening with the Pack." My brogue thickened with my nerves.

"Aye, sis." Colin turned a little in his seat to watch me closer.

"Obviously the Pack isn't happy Dougal's with me since I'm not a werewolf." I cleared my throat. "They also blame me for Duncan and your pa's deaths. It dinnae help that—"

"Your father is dead?" Unna placed her hand on Colin's shoulder. "I can't imagine how that must feel." She glanced between the two of us and cocked her head to the side. "I'm sorry for interrupting. That was rude of me."

Colin sighed and placed his hand over Unna's. "Thanks, love. Truthfully, I can't say I'm upset about the fact. He..." He glanced in my direction, then averted his gaze. "He wasn't a good man."

It was a gross understatement, but I imagined that was about as much as Colin wanted to share and the only thing she really needed to know.

Unna chewed on her lower lip and squeezed his hand before scooting back into the seat. She looked at me, too, as if trying to find what my brother saw, but then she turned her attention back toward the passing scenery again.

"Nae, he wasn't. Being at the funeral didn't help, I guess. A few of the older wolves took offense to it, and a big fight started. Dougal broke it up." The tension in my shoulders was back from talking about it. I rolled my neck to release some of the stress balled up there. "Uh, Kerr..." My throat was scratchy and dry, and I cleared it again.

"Stop beating around the bush, sis. You're not the type of lass to do that. Whatever that bastard did, tell me, or I can't help ye."

Colin was right. I needed to talk to him. "Kerr contacted Dougal's brother, who's probably coming to challenge him. With Kerr being Dougal's second-in-command, Dougal needs someone by his side that he trusts." The words poured out in a rush, and I pulled over at a passing place to catch my breath. No cars were coming. The dark leather steering wheel gave a metallic groan beneath my white knuckles. My hands hurt from squeezing it so hard.

"For fuck's sake. Are ye shittin' me? That bastard is coming back to challenge Dougal?" Colin looked ready to spit. "He'd have to be mad. Kerr's just as bad, if he's siding with a fuckin' coward." Colin sucked in a deep breath, then let it out slowly before taking another. "Ye shouldn't be worrying, sis. That wanker won't do anything." The anxious look he gave me didn't reassure me, though. I could tell he knew this could all come crumbling down on Dougal's head and my own.

Shaking my head, I returned my focus to the road,

putting the Jeep into drive. "Maybe, but I'm scared." I whispered the last word.

Colin squeezed my shoulder, then switched on the radio. The two of us stared at the scenery while Unna played with my brother's phone. We continued without another word for a little over three hours.

"Um," Unna piped up hesitantly. "I need to use the loo."

Colin shrugged. "Aye, it wouldn't hurt to grab lunch too. You're still healing, and we shouldn't get too hungry." He eyed the side mirror for about the twentieth time in the past fifteen minutes. "Wherever we go, make sure it's populous. I think we're being followed."

"Lunch sounds good." The rearview mirror had shown the same dark green sedan behind us for a while, but we were on the A9. The portion we were on was a two-lane road heading toward Edinburgh. They could easily be heading in the same direction. Besides, who in the Pack would be ballsy enough to go after me with Colin around? Who would even know? It made little sense, so I shook the thoughts away. We turned off the highway toward Dalwhinnie.

Unsurprisingly, the green sedan continued down the highway. I let out a soft sigh and returned my attention to finding us a place to eat. Despite the car going past, Colin's idea of finding somewhere with plenty of other people wasn't a bad idea. The thought of werewolves coming after us hadn't occurred to me before, but now the idea made me restless, especially with Unna around. She wiggled in her seat a little and bit her lower lip as if trying to keep from complaining again.

On the side of the road was a decent-sized restaurant and gift shop combo, complete with a tourist bus just about to pull in from the opposite direction. That fit the bill. I pulled in first as the bus driver hesitated, and grabbed a parking spot near the front.

"Let's try to hurry in here," I said. "I'd like to get back on the road as quickly as we can." The sooner that happened, the sooner I could see Dougal again. I thought of sending him a text to let him know what was going on, but I could do that inside.

Colin nodded. "Aye. Good thinking, sis." He held the back passenger door open for Unna and offered her his hand.

My eyebrows shot up. My brother... From scary monster to romantic prince. Who knew?

I locked the door, then headed inside to find us a table before they were all taken. The tour guide was shouting over the loud bagpipe music to his talkative group that they'd be stopping here for an hour and not to stray far. Solid advice. The waitress seated me quickly with a warm smile. "I hope ye dinnae mind. We're expecting lots of guests today. Once the lot of ye ken what you'd like, be sure to get your order in. We had a wee problem with running out of food the last time this many people visited."

"Aye, thanks." I flipped through the menu, seeing several tempting choices. "It shouldn't be long. Waitin' on my brother and his girlfriend."

"I'll be back in a moment then." The waitress smiled again, and I couldn't help but smile back.

A few minutes later, Colin and Unna walked into view hand-in-hand, laughing with each other over something Unna was carrying. When they got to the table, I could see it was a tacky magnet joking about what men wore under their kilts. I rolled my eyes. Ha, ha.

"I'm off to the loo now. I'll have the fish and chips, and a Coke. Order for me if I'm not back. Make up yer mind, because the waitress will be back soon," I said. Actually, she was already looking in our direction, so I waved to her.

The happiness on Colin's face melted into a frown, but he nodded. "Go ahead."

Shite. I didn't want him to think I was a bitch after dragging him away from his retreat. I forced a smile on my face. It wasn't genuine, but Unna smiled back. Awkward. Beyond awkward since I didn't even know how serious they were. Could Unna be his mate? No...Colin would never, not without telling me.

I strode toward the small hallway with the loo, which was in the gift shop section of the building. Apparently, the waitress was right. There were many people here now. Through the front doors, I caught sight of two more tourist buses arriving and wanted to smack myself upside the head for picking this place. Still, Colin wanted somewhere with many people.

An unsettling scent drew my attention in the large crowd, but I couldn't track down what it might be.

An exit door stood slightly ajar at the end of the short corridor, but I shrugged it off and pushed open the restroom door. I entered one of the three stalls, unfastening the button on my jeans. My nose twitched as I caught a whiff of someone in another stall.

The smoky, masculine scent shocked me. I was damn sure I'd chosen the ladies' room. The bathroom door opened and closed, and a faint click signaled the door locking. My heart pounded in my chest, and I buttoned my jeans again, keeping as still and as quiet as I could.

The newcomer's dirty boots appeared under the door directly in front of me, and he inhaled loudly. "Come out, little kitty. We want to play."

The scent that concerned me before came back. Werewolves. Two of them.

Fuckin' shite!

Why hadn't I gone to the loo when Unna went? I stepped away from the door. *Think, Caitlyn. Think!* Colin might be able to get these bastards to back off without drawing much attention. I checked my mobile phone, but its battery was dead. My fist clenched around it, the plastic squeaking under my strength. I shoved the phone in my pocket as a male hand clasped the top of the door.

"I'm not waiting any longer, kitty cat." He pushed. The door's lock snapped, and it flew open, nearly slamming into me.

I braced my palms against the sides of the stall and kicked out with both legs, hitting the man with all my strength. He smacked against the wall opposite the stall. A low growl rumbled from his chest as he shook out his greying hair, the glint of wolf amber shining in his eyes.

I balled my hands into fists, ready to take him on. That wasn't so hard. My leopard purred with pride. I could handle these jerks.

Another male gripped my hair, pulling me straight up. My head ached from holding all of my weight, and I cried out in pain. I grabbed my new assailant's wrist, desperate to relieve the tension on my hair. My nails bit into his flesh, and my beast rumbled in my chest. She rose to the surface, stretching upward from the core of my body. She demanded blood from these pathetic werewolves. If I let her take over, I might lose control.

My grip on my beast faltered, but I shoved her down a little. I could allow her primal instincts to lead my human body, but I couldn't risk shifting near a gift shop full of tourists. What if we broke out of here and someone saw my leopard form? The Pard was just as strict as the Pack when it came to revealing ourselves, and I really didn't want trouble with my werecat overlords.

My nails lengthened into claws, and I sank them into my attacker's wrist as Grey pushed himself up from the wall and grinned at me as if he were a shark and I was bait.

The arsehole holding me sank his sharp canine teeth into

my fingers. Someone apparently spent too much time in their animal form. My heart skipped a beat as my thoughts flashed to the funeral, and the older wolf who'd picked a fight with me. Could this be the same guy?

Grey sauntered toward me as if he was tough shit, then swung his fist at me. I barely twisted out of the way, feeling his rough knuckles slide across my stomach instead of pounding into it. My scalp continued to throb from carrying my weight. If I didn't get the other arsehole off me, I'd just be a punching bag for Grey. He didn't seem too smart, but sooner or later, he'd get to work on beating the shite out of me.

An idea clicked in my head, and I ran up the stall's wall, flipping into the adjoining loo with the asshole pulling my hair. Just as I'd suspected, he was the wanker from the funeral. That bastard! He looked different without his kilt and proper hygiene.

I landed on his shoulders with my feet dangling down his back. His mouth dropped open, and he widened his eyes at me, as if stunned that I'd outmaneuvered him. His grip on my hair slipped a little, giving me a chance to free myself. I hammered punches into his mouth, feeling his sharp teeth slice into my knuckles.

The brute slammed me into the wall above the toilet, and my teeth rattled from the impact. Some of the tiles clattered to the floor around us, and I squeezed my thighs around the bastard's neck trying to choke him out before he did more damage. His face was turning red, but he grinned like a maniac, clearly enjoying this. He grabbed me by the throat and slapped my head back into the wall. More ceramic shattered on the floor, and I grabbed his wrist. When I thought he'd do it again, Grey appeared over his shoulder.

"Fucking hell, George. You can't have all the fun. I need a turn at the feisty lass."

George lifted me in the air without breaking a sweat and turned me toward his friend. My stomach lurched as he slammed me down with my head hanging at an awkward angle. Stars exploded behind my eyes, and pain spiked through my skull as it hit the floor. I fought to remain conscious. Thankfully my shoulders had taken some of the impact, but not nearly enough.

I pushed my thighs together even more, letting the strength of my leopard assist me. I tried rotating my hips in hopes of getting a better angle, but it didn't seem to help much. My beast roared at me to let go and accept the shift, but I refused. If someone came in here when I was in leopard form… It was way too dangerous.

George grabbed my thighs, trying to pry my legs off of him. With his brutish strength, if given enough time, I was pretty sure he'd succeed.

Grey fisted his meaty hand into my hair and slammed his fist into my face. I tried to shield myself against his punishing blows. He wasn't as weak as I'd thought he would be. My distraction with him gave George the upper hand, and he threw me to the ground, free from my legs.

I hit the tiles hard. The breath exploded from my lungs, and I gasped, trying to roll onto my side and catch my breath. George pinned me to the floor, keeping me on my back with one hand against my shoulder.

"F-fuck off. Why are ye d-doing this?" My voice cracked as I tried to form the words in between gasps.

"You should've kept that puss in yer pants, lassie. The Scottish Pack dinnae need yer feline kind getting our Alpha confused," George said.

"Must be quite something if our laird likes it, though." A dark twinkle filled Grey's eyes, but George slapped him on the back of the head.

"There are far better choices out there. Even a human

would be better than that." George looked like he wanted to spit. His rancor and venom would've brought tears to my eyes if I wasn't fighting for my life. How could he say such a thing?

"Aye, I know." Grey stared down at me with that darkness lingering in his gaze.

My heart raced. If I didn't do something, I might not make it out of here. The thought of never seeing Dougal again stirred a fire in my belly, but the blows to my head made my arms and legs feel incredibly heavy. I needed to fight through this.

George cocked back his fist and slammed it into my stomach.

The ferocity of each punch knocked my air out again, leaving me gasping for oxygen. Dark spots clouded my vision, and the need to let go as my leopard demanded was becoming more overpowering.

Grey bashed my head into the floor a few times. "Seems she's learning her place. I liked her better when she was feisty."

"Fuck you," I hissed, twisting my body to protect my stomach and figure out how to get out of this. I kicked George in the knee as he lifted his arm for another punch.

The bulk of his weight landed on top of me before I could roll out of the way. He punched me in the jaw as soon as he recovered. The strength of the blow smashed my head into the floor, breaking the tiles.

My ears rattled, and my body weakened. I tried to lift my hands up to shelter myself, but they wouldn't move from my sides. I wanted to fight back and prove the mistake they'd made when they decided to pick on me, but my body didn't want to cooperate. For the third time in my life, I felt like the helpless little girl that Alistair abused. Tears burned my eyes.

Just when I was about to give up, a soft knock on the door

made me moan. I reached for the door. If someone was there, I could get help. I could get away from these werewolves. I opened my mouth to scream, but Grey's fat fingers pressed firmly against my lips. Darkness began to close in, and I didn't have the strength to do much more than groan.

The doorknob jiggled a little, but I heard footsteps heading away a few moments later. My hopes of being saved fizzled, and I narrowed my eyes at the cocky man in front of me.

George pulled back his fist with a grin.

11

COLIN

"There are so many people in here, Colin." Unna leaned closer. "I've never seen this many before." She wrapped her small hand around my own. "They have so many different accents, too."

"It's a tour group, love. They're on holiday to see Scotland." I squeezed her hand softly, trying to give her moral support, but she didn't seem to be scared, only curious. The sound of so many people talking grated on my nerves. I couldn't take much more. A headache built within my skull, and I pushed my fingers against my temples. I'd never been agoraphobic, but it'd been a while since I'd been around this many people.

Perhaps Caitlyn had followed my suggestion a little too well. I'd thought of a slightly smaller place with just enough people, not this kind of chaos. My beast scratched at the surface, feeling my pain, and my grip on Unna's hand tightened a little. Her presence soothed my beast, and right now, she was the only thing holding him off.

I drummed the fingers of my other hand against the table

as I stared into the horde of people moving through the gift shop.

Our waitress arrived with three plates of fish and chips, giving us a kind smile. "Here ye are. Enjoy. If ye need anything else, let me know."

I nodded my head but kept my attention on the crowd.

Unna started digging into her chips. She stopped after a few bites and frowned, noticing that I wasn't even looking at my own food.

Something didn't feel right. Why wasn't Caitlyn back yet?

"Should we wait for your sister?" Unna placed her hand on my arm, and I nearly jumped at the soft touch. "If you want, I could go check to see if she's okay." Unna gave me a bright smile, and I couldn't help but smile back.

If Caitlyn were in trouble, I hated the thought of sending Unna after her. The sweet lass didn't have the same ability to protect herself as Caitlyn did. But I could be overreacting. Caitlyn was dealing with enough, with having found a mate and her world being turned upside down by the Pack. I didn't want to barge in if she had an upset stomach.

"Aye, love. I'd appreciate that." I brushed my thumb over Unna's hand, then pulled back. Unna waded through the crowd of people as cheerful as ever. My stomach turned as I stared down at the food, now starting to get cold. Hunger was the least of my concerns at the moment. A few minutes passed with no signs of Unna. Just as I was about to go check on her too, she was striding back toward me. Concern paled her fair skin, and I jerked to my feet, almost knocking over my chair. "What's going on?"

"The door was locked, so I knocked on it. No one answered. I'm worried. You should go see about her." Her breath came out in soft pants, and she nudged me toward the gift shop. "I don't think all is well."

For fuck's sake. Hopefully, this was all a

misunderstanding, and Caitlyn just needed her privacy. It'd certainly be understandable, but my sister didn't do things like this. It felt wrong. "Ask the waitress if we can get our food to go," I said, trying to remain calm. I walked to the ladies' room I'd escorted Unna to earlier.

Part of me wasn't comfortable doing this. If I was blowing this out of proportion, I might escalate the tension with my sister more. I didn't want to do that. The door to the ladies' room was tucked down a hallway toward a storage area. I stood in front of it, steeling my resolve to knock, when my nose caught a surprising scent. Werewolf? *Och, the fuck?* The sound of knuckles pounding into flesh sent the hair on the back of my neck standing up. I took a deep breath, zeroing in on what I'd smelled before—two male werewolves were in there with Caitlyn.

I kicked open the door, not caring about the people meandering around the gift shop mere feet away. The small, purple-tinted restroom was a complete mess: the door to one stall was leaning against the opposite wall and bits of broken tile were everywhere.

Two werewolves leaned over Caitlyn, smashing their fists into her face and stomach. Both were older men, and the larger one looked familiar. I couldn't place where I'd seen him, though. Blood pooled around my sister, who lay limp on the tile floor with her arms at her sides, unresponsive to the blows.

A low, vicious growl ripped from my throat as I stepped inside, shutting the door behind me. These men would pay with their lives for treating my sister like that. You don't fuck with family. I cracked my knuckles and took a few steps forward. My beast slammed against the surface of my skin, drawn forth by my rage and the coppery scent of blood.

The floor rose up to greet me as my legs gave way, and I fell to my hands and knees. My fingers bit into the floor, breaking tiles with the strength of my beast as he bent my human form to his superior shape. My fingers stretched into claws, and my eyesight sharpened as I looked at them with my wolf's eyes.

The two men backed away from Caitlyn with wide, startled eyes. "We have no quarrel with you," the larger man said. "We were just after her." He lifted his arms in surrender, but my beast and I could smell his fear. We enjoyed the scent.

I didn't answer. We stalked forward on our hands and knees. It might've been an awkward position for a human, but I wasn't human...not fully. It felt natural just then.

"Let's get the fuck out of here, George. He's about to shift, and I don't want to catch shite for him wreaking havoc in a gift shop full of people." Grey dodged to my left while George scrambled to my right to escape. We raked our long claws over his chest as a growl erupted from our throat. The men threw open the door and ran. I looked down at my sister. If it wasn't for our heightened sense of hearing, I might've missed the fact she was breathing.

The door shut, and I tensed, ready to rip out the throat of whoever was invading this moment. A snarl trickled from my throat. George's friend was right. I was a ticking time bomb, and quite frankly, I didn't care if I exploded. My heart ached for my sister, and my beast raged at me for letting this happen.

Unna's soft gasp drew my gaze to meet hers. She had her hand against her mouth. Her blue eyes were wide with shock but not fear. I took a deep breath, focusing on her aquatic scent. She glanced between me and Caitlyn, concern etched in her face. "Is...is she okay?"

I tried to talk, but a growl rumbled from my throat instead, so I shook my head. My beast had a tight hold on my body. He still fought to fully shift instead of remaining in between forms.

She walked closer carefully, as if easing her way through a minefield. The slightest scent of fear wafted from her, and it took all my strength not to bare my teeth at her. *Mate.* She knelt beside me and ran her hand through my still-human hair. Her touch soothed the raw beast threatening to rip this place apart in anger. "We need to get out of here, Colin. Please don't become lost to me." She cupped my face and pressed a gentle kiss to my lips. "You're all I have now." She tilted her head toward my sister. "You're all she has right now, too. Come back to us."

I closed my eyes, concentrating on her words and the feeling of her hands on my face. I let that anchor me, fighting back the beast. With Unna's presence and the men gone, he wasn't as adamant to take a stand. I wrapped my arms around Unna and buried my nose into the crook of her neck, breathing in her scent deeply. My claws slid back into my hands, and my eyesight shifted back to normal. "Thank ye."

Unna squeezed me tighter, then pushed to her feet. She glanced around me at the bathroom. "We really should leave. A line of women was forming outside, and they didn't look too happy." She bit her lower lip.

"Go get the food." I handed her enough money to cover the meal. "Meet me at the car. I'll bring Caitlyn directly there."

Unna nodded. She opened the door, pushing past a few women on the way out who stared into the lasses' room. One woman seemed to scramble in her purse for something.

"Nae need. She's my sister. I'm takin' her to the doctor." I lifted Caitlyn into my arms gently, cradling her neck.

"Are you sure you should move her? What even happened to her?" the woman asked.

"It must've been those big guys who were in there too," another woman from further down the line said. "They had blood on them."

"Aye, it was," I replied feeling a little uncomfortable with the press of people in the tight hallway. "Sorry for the wait, lasses."

A few of the waiting women just smiled at me with curiosity in their eyes. Right.

I glanced toward the front door and the mass of people there. Even more people would react to Caitlyn's condition and the fact that I was carrying her away. I looked at the other end of the hall past the men's room and spotted an exit sign. I pushed it open with my shoulder, breathing a sigh of relief in the crisp air. The Jeep was in front, so I jogged around the building and laid Caitlyn in the back seat. I slid my jacket off and placed it over her torso to help keep her warm. She groaned a little, and I let out a breath I hadn't known I was holding.

Unna's hurried footsteps drew my attention as she walked around the Jeep to the passenger side. "Um. Where should I sit? Do you want me to be back there with her to—"

"Nae. Sit in the front." I reached into Caitlyn's pocket and pulled the car keys out. "I don't want to risk her accidentally attacking ye."

Unna's eyes widened, but she did as I said. She put on her seatbelt and looked straight ahead. "You really think she'd hurt me?" She chewed on her lower lip, squirming a little in her seat.

I stuck the keys in the ignition and pulled away from the parking spot. "Calm yerself, love. She's badly hurt and healing, which means she's not her normal self. It's a precaution." I squeezed her hand, not sure who needed the comfort more, her or me.

No one appeared to be running out of the gift shop after us. At least that was something. I turned onto the main road heading toward the highway again. "I should ring my Alpha, her mate. He needs to know about this." My mobile wasn't in my jean pockets like usual. Had I left it at the restaurant in my hurry?

Unna held it up. "You gave it to me so I could play that card game on your phone during the drive." She blushed. "I think you'll have to show me how to play. I'm not very good at solitary."

"Solitaire." The memory came back then—I'd given it to her before we left the cottage.

I dialed Dougal's number, and the phone rang a few times before he picked up.

"Hell—"

"Caitlyn's injured. We're still a couple hours away from Edinburgh." There wasn't time for niceties, not when my sister was barely moving in the backseat.

"What the bloody hell? I want to talk to her! Now!" Dougal switched from the friend who'd answered the phone to full-on Alpha mode.

"She's unconscious, you shite."

Unna widened her eyes. Her lower lip trembled. "That's how you speak to your Alpha?"

"Who was that?" Dougal's voice lowered into a growl.

I clenched my hand into a fist around the steering wheel, wishing Unna hadn't chimed in. This was the last thing Dougal needed to hear. "That's my mate. She's with us." I frowned at her, and she glanced out the side window. "She's a selkie."

"For fuck's sake, man." The line was silent for a few moments, and I almost wondered if he'd disconnected the call. A ragged sigh finally came over the line. "What happened to Caitlyn? How did she get injured?"

"We made a stop for lunch. She went to use the loo and was attacked by two male werewolves." I pulled onto the side of the road and stopped. "She did some damage to them too, but she's in bad shape. I thought I recognized one of them, but I have no idea where from."

"Bloody hell."

I twisted in the seat to look at Caitlyn, who was still unconscious. Her eyes were closed, and she would have looked peaceful if it wasn't for the blood and bruises all over her face. "When I barged in, they fled, saying they had no ill will with me. They seemed scared I'd kill everyone around us."

"Come again?" Dougal started coughing, almost violently. "There were people around?"

"Outside of the loo. We were inside. With the door shut."

"Small miracles, aye? Damn." He sounded utterly exhausted now. "I'll ring you back. Let me call a friend who lives nearby. I'll text you the directions. Caitlyn should recuperate a bit before coming back. The threat here might be worse than out there. I wouldn't want someone taking advantage of her weak state. I'll send the Pack's doctor, Roy, up to look over her. I still trust him…" Under his breath, I swore I heard him say, "I think." He cleared his throat. "Please take care of Caitlyn. I ask that not only as your Alpha, but as a friend and her mate." His voice trembled a little at the last word. I knew how hard it was for him to keep it together. If it hadn't been for Unna, I had no idea what I would've done.

"Aye, I will." With that, I ended the call and tossed the mobile in the center console. I rested my forehead on the steering wheel, waiting for the text.

12

UNNA

"Are you okay?" I ran my hand over Colin's back in soothing circles. From what I'd seen in the restroom, he'd been about to lose himself to his beast again. That terrified me so badly. What would happen if he totally lost touch with himself? Would he have killed the people in the gift shop? Would he have killed me? My heart rate sped up a little, but he'd be able to pick up my fear, so I took a deep breath. Just when I'd thought he was regaining his humanity again, this happened.

Colin frowned at me. "I'm trying to be." He sighed and placed his forehead back against the steering wheel. "I'm sorry about earlier, in the restroom. It's tough seeing her in that condition." He balled his hands into fists in his lap, his arms shaking from the effort to keep them still.

"It's...understandable." I smiled at him, trying to be the soothing, loving mate he needed right now. "Anyone would have reacted the same if their sibling was hurt." I wasn't sure if that was true, or how I would act in his case. My only siblings came from my father's new relationship, and we weren't close.

The phone beeped between us, and I picked it up carefully. "He sent the text message."

Colin leaned back in the seat and started the engine. "Aye, what does it say?"

"It says, 'I've called a member who lives nearby. He will take you in to let Caitlyn recover before you continue your journey with Roy's supervision. He has a patient to look after tonight, but he'll be there first thing in the morning.' It also has an address." I held the phone out to him, and he messed with it a little before a woman's voice came out, saying, "Go straight for three kilometers."

I cocked my head to the side at the phone. "Is someone in there? She sounds a little strange."

Colin smiled at me, but the look didn't reach his eyes. "The woman isnae real. She's a computerized voice. The phone is telling us how to get there."

"Okay." A computerized voice that told directions. What else would they think of? Part of me felt entirely out of my depth being on solid ground, especially now.

I glanced into the back seat at Colin's sister. Her face was bloody and swollen. Pity rose in my chest, and I wished there was something more I could do for her. She'd seemed nice, and I only hoped she lived long enough for us to get to know one another.

Colin patted my thigh, drawing my attention back to him. "She'll be okay. She's been through worse."

My eyes widened, and I looked back to her before meeting his gaze. "Worse than this?" A chill chased down my spine, and I shivered.

"Aye, lass." He sighed heavily. "She's a survivor."

I chewed on my lower lip, wondering what kind of life the siblings had experienced. I wasn't sure if I wanted to know. We made the rest of the trip to the Pack member's house in silence.

A big man with a broad chest and legs thicker than some tree trunks walked outside the wooden house as we pulled up. He waved to us with a kind smile. "Laddie, good to see you again," he said as we stepped out of the car.

Colin smiled back and held out his hand. Instead of a handshake, the big man pulled him in for a hug. "I didn't ken ye lived around here, Hamish. I thought ye lived closer to Glasgow."

Hamish pulled back to grin at Colin. "I moved a few years ago. I didn't fancy the city life anymore. I'm much happier out here." He released Colin, then looked me over. "Who is this lovely lass?"

They looked pretty friendly toward one another, so I mimicked Colin's gesture and held out my hand. "My name is Unna. Colin and I are mates." Hamish took my hand in his and placed a soft kiss to my knuckles. I widened my eyes and looked to Colin. I caught a glint of something dark in his eyes before it disappeared. Had I done something wrong?

Hamish smiled at me. "It's lovely you've finally found your mate, Colin." He opened his mouth as if to say more but stopped himself. "I'm Hamish, lass. Welcome to my home." He glanced in the backseat at last, and a frown curved his lips. "This one doesn't appear to be in good shape. Let's get her inside." He opened the car door, but Colin pushed forward to pull his sister out of the car himself.

"It's okay. I'll carry her," Colin said, forcing a smile. He'd become very protective of her ever since he found her injured. Maybe he felt guilty for not having gotten to her sooner.

"No worries, lad." Hamish closed the car door behind him and led the way into the house. "There's a spare room there." He pointed at the door closest to the living room. "My room is here." He nodded to the next door down. "The bathroom is there, and the last spare room is at the end of the hall."

Colin glanced at each door looking indecisive. "Thanks," he mumbled, heading to the first door near the living room. I opened it for him, and he set Caitlyn down on the bed. "My apologies for the blood. I can give you some money to help—"

Hamish patted Colin on the shoulder. "Nae, don't worry. She's not the first one to come in here bloodied, and I'm sure she won't be the last." He chuckled and shook his head. "There's beer in the fridge, and you can use the oven to heat up your food."

I'd nearly forgotten about our lunch, but now that he reminded us, my stomach growled. "I'll go get it from the car."

Colin nodded and handed me the keys. Then he rolled up his sleeves and headed for the kitchen.

When I got back, Colin was in the bedroom gently wiping the blood off of Caitlyn's face with a damp towel. I left them alone and warmed the food using the tips I'd remembered from Ailsa's book. If I'd been smart, I would've asked for a copy. I hadn't realized life on land would be so complicated, and now that I was with someone else, I didn't want him to think I couldn't do anything for myself. I was determined to prove those negative thoughts wrong.

I reached for the pan in the oven after the food had warmed for a while.

Hamish's chuckle halted my actions. "I think you're forgetting something, lass." He held up two oversized mittens.

For a moment, I frowned at him, trying to recall what those were for, but I quickly remembered the heat burning my fingers the first time I cooked in the oven. "Oh! Thank you." He handed them over, and I slipped them on to get the food out.

"You're different from any lass I've seen before." He

sniffed the air and took a couple steps closer. "You're a selkie, aren't you?"

I jerked my head toward him, almost dropping the cooking sheet. "Wh...what?"

Hamish waved his hand at me. "Don't be shy. I've been around long enough to learn a thing or two about Scottish folklore." The grey patches of hair at his temples were a testament to the truth of what he said, but being alone with him unnerved me now, especially after the fisherman who'd tried to make me his bride. "No need to be afraid." He took a few steps back so that he stood near the kitchen's entrance. "It's just not every day one meets your kind."

"S-sorry. I've just had some bad experiences with people recently when they found out what I am. Some of them remember the tales they heard as a child and want to take advantage of them." I looked down at the food, trying not to think about my mother. This wasn't the time to be feeling sorry for myself and what I'd lost. I took the plates Hamish had set aside for us earlier and arranged the fish and chips on them.

"I can only imagine." He cleared his throat and headed to the fridge, grabbing a beer. "There's more in the fridge if you want some."

"Thanks." I set the food at the table, then went to the spare room where Colin was sitting on the bed by Caitlyn's side. "Is she awake yet?"

He looked at me, and I could see the pain in his eyes a moment before it disappeared. "Nae, she's not." He sniffed the air. "Food's ready?"

I nodded.

Colin glanced between me and Caitlyn, then rose to his feet and headed to the table where we ate. Things had settled down a little. Colin received a couple of text messages that made him kind of grumpy, but we headed off to bed after a while. He had dark circles under his eyes and looked exhausted. I could only imagine how he felt. He'd been through a lot with helping me, and now he was helping Caitlyn without much time to rest. We curled up in one another's arms, and sleep took me over.

It wasn't long before I woke up again. The house was almost pitch black. Only the waxing moon shining in the window lit the room. I looked over to see Colin on his side facing away from me. All of the blankets were covering him, leaving me with nothing. I shivered at the air's coolness and reached over to steal the covers back, but a muffled sound deeper in the house drew my attention.

From Colin's deep breathing, I knew he was still sound asleep. I thought about waking him up, but what if it was my imagination? I didn't want to disturb his sleep just because we were in a new place.

I climbed out of bed, still feeling like I should investigate. Maybe Caitlyn had woken up? She could need help getting to the loo, or maybe she wanted food. It was the least I could do.

Rubbing the sleep from my eyes, I walked down the hall. Hamish's bedroom door was shut, and I shrugged. When I turned into Caitlyn's room, Hamish was standing over her with a pillow pressing into her face. "Wh-what are you doing?" I asked. Surprise and fear held me in place for a moment. Caitlyn's limbs were shaking, but she wasn't fighting back. I had to help her.

Hamish frowned back at me. "Get out of here, lass. I don't want to hurt you."

A scream ripped from my throat as I grabbed the folding chair Colin had been sitting in earlier near the bedside and smacked Hamish on the back of the head with it. He dropped the pillow, then whirled around and wrenched the chair from my hands, tossing it to the side. He punched me in the face, snapping my head back and sending me colliding with the wall near the door.

My body struck hard, and my knees gave way. I slid down the wall, watching helplessly as Hamish wrapped his thick hands around Caitlyn's slender throat as if he couldn't be bothered with the pillow now. If only I'd been stronger, I could have helped her. My vision narrowed, but I tried to push to my feet.

A cool breeze drew my attention to Colin standing in the doorway. He stared at Hamish in shock, where the man loomed over Caitlyn as she unconsciously struggled to stay alive. Then he looked at me. His eyes flashed wolf amber, and his body dropped to the ground, nearly exploding into fur and fangs. The change was so quick and frightening that I couldn't stop myself from crying out. He snarled viciously in his wolf form and lunged at Hamish, knocking the other man across the bed to the other side. They were barely visible from the end of the bed.

"Calm down, lad." Hamish grabbed Colin by the throat, but Colin snapped at his arm, ripping his teeth through Hamish's flesh. "I was a friend of your father's. I don't want to hurt you. That cat girl is nothing but trouble. She has to be dealt with. I... Damn it, Colin! Stop!" He pulled his arm back to punch Colin, but the opening gave Colin the chance to spring for his neck.

"That's Colin's sister," I said, my throat rasping. "By hurting her, you did hurt him." My vision darkened a little more, but I struggled to remain awake, especially now. I didn't want Colin to be left alone trying to defend himself against Hamish. My body slumped a little more. I couldn't see what was happening anymore, but the sounds were horrifying.

Thick gurgling and wheezing gasps of air filled the quiet room, along with rumbling snarls. I pressed my hands over my ears, trying to block out the noise. After a moment, the room went eerily silent except for harsh breathing.

I looked up to see Colin padding toward me in his wolf form, blood staining his muzzle and chest. I did my best not to curl up into a ball and pretend to be invisible. He wouldn't hurt me. I knew he wouldn't...

Colin whimpered and nuzzled my hand, then laid his head in my lap. Sadness and love for him ached in my chest. I ran my hand over his furry head in short strokes. Colin didn't like to be petted, but he seemed to need the comfort now. Even as my body weakened, I waited, hoping he'd shift back to his human form any time now, but he didn't. Or... maybe he couldn't?

Those thoughts drifted away as the darkness weighing against me could no longer be suppressed. My vision faded, and the world turned dark like the sea.

COLIN

*E*very nerve in my body tensed as Unna went limp and flopped against me. My wolf whimpered again, and we nudged her in hopes she'd wake up. I needed to shift back to human form if I had a prayer of helping Unna and Caitlyn, but the explosive shift to wolf form had terrified me both as man and beast. The bastard's bullshit reasons and story about being my father's friend didn't ease my mind one bit. If I could, I would kill him all over again to release the fury boiling within me. We licked Unna's cheek to try to rouse her, but she wouldn't wake up. The position she lay in didn't look comfortable, and I needed to be there to care for my mate.

Focusing inward, I fought to push back the beast, but he resisted me. After a few deep breaths, I concentrated harder on the change until my wolf finally retreated in our battle of wills. He growled at me but submitted.

Our claws withdrew back into my skin, and the fur covering my hands disappeared. I huffed out a sigh of relief. The fact I'd gained strength over my wolf sparked a rush of victory inside me. Perhaps the months I'd spent cooped up like an animal were finally melting away. The scars would remain, but I had new hope with Unna in my life.

I lifted her into my arms, cradling her neck gently, not knowing how much damage she'd sustained. Her limp body stirred more anger in me. I placed her on the bed next to Caitlyn, even though I was a little hesitant about that. If Caitlyn changed or reacted like an animal in her injured state, I didn't want her to hurt Unna. I'd been stupid not to look after them better, and I'd almost lost my sister.

Tears burned the back of my eyes, but I didn't let them fall. Right now, I couldn't afford weakness. The folded chair laid at the foot of the bed, and I set it beside Unna. Hamish's body blocked my sister's bedside, and the only way for me to sit beside her would be moving him. Even looking at the bastard was painful, and I didn't want to put myself through that.

Dougal would want to know about this new assault, but I didn't know how to tell him that I'd almost let my sister, his mate, be killed by some arsehole he'd trusted and whom I used to know. I'd let my fuckin' guard down and almost paid a dear price. The two women rested on the bed, still and battered. My hands balled into fists.

Hamish's offer of the beer in his fridge came back to me. Drinking to numb my pain had become almost second nature in Durness before I'd met Unna. I stood and was at the door before I could control myself. My fist slammed into the door frame, causing the wood to splinter. Alcohol wouldn't solve this. It'd only lower my guard even more. I needed to remain in control.

Instead of heading for the fridge, I brewed a pot of coffee. The clock read two in the morning, and I doubted I'd get any more sleep. The best thing I could do was watch over the girls and wait for Roy to arrive.

Minutes ticked by on an annoying wall clock, which I

nearly ripped from the wall and tore in two. The crunch of gravel on the driveway jolted me up from the folding chair. My hands trembled from having consumed four pots of strong coffee as I opened the door and walked down the steps to him. Now the clock said it was eight. My heart beat faster than normal, but I couldn't tell if it was from the caffeine or my anxiety over the doctor's arrival.

"Colin," Roy said, looking me over. My shirt and pants were ripped from the change, and drops of blood dotted my clothes. Damn. I hadn't noticed that before. "Something happened last night, didn't it? Where are Hamish and Caitlyn? Is everyone okay?"

I grimaced and shook my head. "Nae, the fuckin' arse tried to kill Caitlyn in the middle of the night." My hands balled into fists, and I pressed them into my sides trying to keep from doing anything stupid.

"What?" Roy pushed past me and ran into the house. His chin lifted as he sniffed loudly, dashing to the bedroom where Caitlyn and Unna lay on the bed with Hamish dead on the floor beside them. He came up short at the sight. "D-did you report this to Dougal?" His voice cracked a little. "This isn't good."

"I told him Caitlyn was injured yesterday. That's why he decided we should stay with Hamish, and why he sent you." Only when no one else came into the room did I realize Roy was alone. "You're by yerself? There's no one to guard ye?"

"No, I'm not." He looked at me pointedly. "You're here."

My mouth nearly dropped open, and I leaned against the broken door frame. What? Couldn't he see that I shouldn't be trusted with everyone's safety? I hadn't been able to protect my sister and my mate. I was far from the best choice. *Bloody hell.*

Roy stepped over Hamish to look at Caitlyn. The beast within me rumbled, but we knew the doctor. He could be trusted. He'd been extremely loyal to Dougal's father, too. From what I'd witnessed, Roy stuck with his Hippocratic Oath, regardless of whether the person deserved his care or not. He glanced up at me standing in the doorway. "Don't linger. Make yourself useful." He tossed his car keys to me. "Get my doctor's bag from the trunk."

The keys slapped my chest, bringing me back to the present, and I caught them. Remain in the present. This wasn't the time to think about what I'd failed to do. I started to turn.

"Grab the tracksuit from the trunk as well while you're at it," Roy said. "You need to change your clothes before we leave, and I don't think Hamish's clothes would fit well."

No, they probably wouldn't. While all Pack members tended to have extra sweats in case they were needed, Hamish had been a mountain of a man. Tall, wide, and full of muscle. If he hadn't tried to avoid hurting me, I doubt I would've killed him so easily. "Aye, doc. I'll be right back."

I kept a close eye on my surroundings as I walked outside. I didn't want any humans to see me in my current shape, and more importantly, I didn't know if Hamish had been plotting his attempt to kill Caitlyn with anyone else. Everyone was a suspect in my eyes now, especially combined with her injury at the gift shop. The tracksuit was in a plastic bag beside the doctor's bag, so I grabbed them both and locked up the car before heading back inside.

The doctor barely looked up when I walked back in, setting his bag at the foot of the bed. "Thanks, lad. Who is that young lass?" He nodded to Unna. "There's something different about the girl."

"Aye," I said, walking over to stand beside her. "She's a selkie and my mate. I told Dougal about her yesterday afternoon after the attack."

Roy lifted his eyebrows at me. "A selkie...is your mate?

Not something you hear every day, I suppose." He cleared his throat and blinked after a few moments, as if snapping out of his shock. "I suspect Dougal didn't take the news well?"

I nodded. "Nae, he didn't. I don't care. She makes me feel alive again. Like I'm not a monster...like I'm a man. Och, that's worth more than anyone else's bloody opinion."

Roy smiled, the expression lighting up his eyes. "Good lad. That's the spirit." His gaze dropped to Caitlyn. "Aside from your sister. Sadly, they're the exception to the rule." His smile faltered, but he continued to look over her wounds.

Dougal had the Pack to look after, but they cared deeply for one another. That should count for something. "Why do they have to be? You're married to a human female. No one cares that female werewolves are scarce when we're mating with humans, but the moment a werewolf falls for another species of shifter or supernatural being, it's like the sky is falling. Wolves are outraged about it. The other Pack I was in despised a witch who was with a new werewolf."

Roy's frown intensified, but he opened his bag and went to work on cleaning the many, now smaller, cuts on Caitlyn's face and neck. "The reason is simple. Wolves, like many others, are afraid of the unknown. Humans are easy to handle. When a werewolf mates with a human, the child will be either werewolf or human. Either case is acceptable. The few known cases of a wolf mating with another shifter have been concerning. In one case, the child was the second shifter's race instead of a wolf. That's fine enough, but other cases..." He sighed and shook his head. "The children ended up being aberrations, and they were ultimately put down for their own good."

My eyes widened, and my legs weakened beneath me. I sat in the folding chair behind me before I fell down. If what he said was true, those fears were founded. This wasn't common knowledge within any Pack I'd been part of, but perhaps it should be. I closed my mouth and opened it again, trying to say something—anything—but no words came out. I could only sit back and let what I'd heard sink in.

"Does Dougal know?" I finally said, finding my voice again.

Roy stopped what he was doing and met my gaze. "No, he's had enough on his plate. I didn't think the news would go over well. I've tried to convince him that he should do what's best for the Pack, but I never wanted him to think I was trying to block him from being with his mate. Unlike some of the others, I feel for him. I've seen the two of them together, and the emotions they have for one another. It's a beautiful thing. Separating mates is not something to be taken lightly."

"Aye. But what about the heartache they'd have to bear if they had to..." I couldn't finish the sentence. It made me think of my relationship with Unna. "Would that affect me and my lass?"

"There's no way to truly know. Selkies, from what I recall as a boy, are more magical creatures. She doesn't derive her ability to shift from the same innate source that we do. She shifts using her pelt, correct?" He looked like he was about to scratch his chin, but blood covered his gloves, so he stopped himself.

I nodded in reply. "Aye, she has a pelt." What he said was true, we were different. But would it be enough when...*if* we had children? The thought of having to kill them for being different ripped me to shreds. I couldn't take the possibility of that being my future. Maybe Unna and I needed to talk about this, but that would rip open other fears. Would she leave me and go back to the ocean with her own kind? I balled my hands into fists. It might be inevitable if I didn't figure out how to break the seven-year spell, but I didn't want to lose her forever because of a topic like this.

Roy looked at me, then down at Unna. "Don't tie yourself in knots about it, lad. I doubt either of you are ready for that step in your lives yet." He sighed and placed another bandage against Caitlyn's cheek. "You'll cross that bridge when you get to it." He nodded to Unna. "Tell me what happened with her. It's plain to see what damage has been done to Dougal's lass."

"What I saw is... My sis... Hamish tried to strangle Caitlyn with his bare hands after smacking Unna into a wall." I nodded toward the blood stain on the wall behind me. "It looks like she hit her head hard." My hands balled into fists, but I straightened my fingers and ran my knuckles over Unna's cheek near the wound Hamish had created with his punch.

The doctor nodded. "I see. I suspect Unna doesn't have the benefit of supernatural healing like a normal shifter?"

Shite, I didn't know what her healing capabilities were like. Had I brought her into a situation where she wouldn't be able to survive? Had I doomed her because I wanted to help my sister and her mate...my current Alpha? I opened my mouth to reply, but Unna cracked open her eyes.

A loving expression softened her face as she stared up at me. She brought her small hand up to caress my face, then jerked her head toward Roy and Caitlyn next to her. The quick motion made her visibly wince, and she curled onto her side, cradling her head. "Colin, is that the doctor?"

"Aye, it is. Rest, love."

Roy frowned at me, then took off his gloves. "If you could grab the body bag and put Hamish in the car's boot, that would be helpful." He grabbed a folded black bag from his doctor's bag and dropped it onto the end of the bed.

I didn't want to leave the two of them there alone. That had caused enough problems on this trip so far: the loo break with Caitlyn, and now having them injured by Hamish. But I needed to trust that Roy was loyal and wouldn't put them in danger.

Instead of protesting, I unfolded the bag beside the big oaf before rolling his body into it. I didn't care about doing the best job at handling a former Pack member's body. He'd forced me to kill him by attacking the two women that meant something to me in this world.

The moment I stepped outside with the body bag, I could smell something in the air that put me on edge. The scent of the two wolves from the restroom came to me. I almost dropped Hamish's body, but the smell was faint now, as if they'd come by but were scared away by the doctor's vehicle.

I opened the trunk and dumped the body inside before slamming the lid. We couldn't remain here much longer. I didn't know how much of a fighter Roy was, but if we were caught off-guard again, I doubted we'd all make it out alive.

14

DOUGAL

"Where the bloody hell are they?" I paced the length of my study. The view of the driveway was unimpeded, and it was the one place I could be alone. I allowed no other wolves into my private sanctuary uninvited. My hands clenched and unclenched at my sides. Roy was supposed to arrive early this morning and bring them immediately here. Hamish's house wasn't far. I'd been there, so I couldn't understand the delay.

On top of all that, Colin wasn't answering my text messages, and I was about to ring the bastard when I saw my Jeep at the end of the driveway. I strode to the window for a better look. Colin was in the driver's seat with a blonde lass beside him. The doctor's car appeared shortly after. My breath hitched in my throat when I didn't see Caitlyn in the passenger seat of Roy's car. Where was she? There had to be a reason behind this. Did she leave after getting beaten up? That made little sense, though.

I walked down the hall to the front door, forcing myself to take evenly paced, deliberate steps when everything within me wanted to run to see what was happening. A few wolves passed me on the way. A couple looked at me with pity, while the last one sneered.

If all went well with my brother's visit, I would be setting the Pack's attitude straight. I refused to take their hatred or their pity. I curled my lips back at the wolf, and he scampered away, apparently not wanting to test if I'd blow my lid at him. He was damned lucky I didn't. I was far from being in the mood for taking shite from anyone.

I threw open the door and leapt down the stairs in one bounce. The brisk morning air stung my cheeks, but nothing else mattered, not when it felt like my heart would explode from my chest if I couldn't find Caitlyn. I looked in the back of my Jeep for Caitlyn before it even stopped, but she wasn't there. A low rumbling growl erupted from my throat, and I headed for the driver's side door. Where was she? Colin had some explaining to do.

Roy opened his door and cleared his throat. "Laird, please calm down. She's over here." He nodded toward his car, where I spotted a still figure in the vehicle's back seat I hadn't noticed before.

My heart raced, but I took calm steps toward the vehicle, doing my best to stay in control. The hair on the back of my neck stood as I felt the Pack's watchful eyes on me. If I lost it, I would further lose their respect. I couldn't have that with my brother's visit so near.

Roy opened the car door and gently lifted her into his arms. He didn't look powerful, but as a werewolf, he was capable of feats even the strongest humans couldn't manage.

My heart dropped to the pit of my stomach when I saw Caitlyn. Bandages littered her bruised and swollen face, and an angry set of handprints circled her delicate neck. I stumbled backward, leaning against my Jeep's bumper. When Colin said she'd been injured, I never imagined it was this bad. This was worse than her run-in with Alistair. I opened my mouth to say something, but no words came out.

Roy carefully cradled her neck, and she still didn't move. She wasn't conscious. That explained why I hadn't heard from her. For a wereleopard to be unconscious was bad news. My heart hammered against the walls of my chest, and I drew a few deep breaths to try to calm myself. I couldn't let myself be so distraught. If I didn't get a handle on my emotions, I'd end up hurting someone.

Gravel crunched behind me, and I looked to see Colin supporting the young blonde female—his selkie mate. I grimaced, but then shook the expression from my face. The last thing I needed was to get into a fight with him. Colin kept his watchful gaze on the doctor, as if ready to catch his sister at any minute if Roy dropped her. He was on edge, and nearly vibrating with energy. The blonde lass ran her hand soothingly over his. That appeared to calm him, but not by much. He looked about ready to lose control. From the lass's cautious stare, I was guessing he probably already had.

"What the bloody hell happened?" I asked.

Colin grimaced and looked behind him at the few wolves standing and staring at us from the front steps, likely wondering what was happening. "It's better to talk about this in private."

"Aye, it is," Roy piped up. "There's someone else that will need to be dealt with." He nodded to the boot of his car.

Blinking slowly, I glanced between the two of them, trying to wrap my mind around what was going on. Then I narrowed my eyes. "Are you saying—"

"Laird, apologies, but as Colin said, it's better to talk elsewhere. Let's go." He started to walk past me carrying Caitlyn, but I stopped him and took her slight weight in my arms instead. She was completely limp, and a little cool to the touch. If not for the fact that I could faintly hear her breathing, I would've lost all control. Roy turned and fetched his bag from the passenger seat.

I stalked toward the front door to the castle, and the group on the steps parted like the Red Sea. My chambers would be the safest place for Caitlyn in her weakened state. I needed her to open her eyes. If she did that, I'd feel a whole helluva lot better. That would bring her back to me. For now, I just wanted to hold her tight and keep her safe.

We walked up the steps, to the second floor of the castle and my chambers. The wolves we encountered gave us a wide berth as we passed. Shock was etched on many of their faces. Very few appeared happy at seeing Caitlyn this hurt. I kept track of those who did and promised to make them pay for disrespecting my mate in her weakened state when I had a chance.

I set Caitlyn on the large bed and ran my hand gently over her dark hair, placing a light kiss to her forehead. "Hang in there, love."

Colin and his mate stood near the TV at the foot of the bed while the doctor edged past me to lay a blanket over Caitlyn and do his usual fussing.

"Tell me what happened." My voice was quiet, like the calm before the storm.

Colin wrapped his arm tighter around his lass as if he could shelter her from the blast with his arms. "We stopped for lunch at a restaurant with a large gift shop. I'd told Caitlyn we should pick someplace with people, because I was sure we were being followed. She followed my advice and picked a spot with some tourist buses, very crowded and busy. She got a table for us, and then when I got back from accompanying Unna to the lasses' room, she needed to use the loo as well." He let out a ragged breath. "She was there for a while, so Unna went to check on her. Unna told me the door was locked, and she couldn't hear anything from inside, so I went to double-check what was going on. I didn't want to intrude if she was sick, but I was worried about her, especially after thinking someone was following us."

I frowned at him.

"I smelled the werewolves then, and I kicked open the door. One of them seemed familiar. He was an older, tall, bulky guy. Both were beating her. I nearly lost control. If it hadn't been for Unna, I would have." Colin placed a kiss to the top of the lass's head. "She helped me regain my sanity, and we took Caitlyn to the Jeep, where I called ye. Ye told us to visit Hamish, and that bloody bastard..." He took a few deep breaths and let them out slowly. His face took on a reddish tint, and Unna brought her small hand up to stroke his chest, which seemed to pull Colin a little bit back from the dark place he'd been.

Unna looked up at me with her big, innocent blue eyes. "Hamish was friendly at first, but I walked in on him trying to smother Caitlyn with a pillow. He punched me when I tried to help her, and then he went to strangle her with his hands. He said he was a good friend of Colin's father." She frowned and returned her gaze to Colin. "Colin did what he had to do and killed Hamish."

Colin nodded once, his jaw tense.

"Damn." I clenched my hands into fists until my knuckles hurt. "I never would have sent you to him if I'd known that." I'd royally screwed up and nearly gotten my mate killed. How could I live with myself? Nausea rose from my stomach.

Movement outside the window drew my eye, and I turned to see a sports car pulling into the long driveway. I'd never seen that vehicle, and we didn't get random strangers. The car drove up to the circle down below, and my breath caught in my throat as my brother stepped out. That bastard. He was days early. He always had the worst timing.

Colin stepped up beside me and looked out the window

too. A low growl rumbled in his chest before he stopped himself. "Shite. He's here."

Roy paused what he was doing and turned to look at us. "You need to go meet him, Dougal. Face the situation head-on. If you don't, he'll have that much more power over your people." He was right. I hated it, but I couldn't just stand around at the window and hide from Ewan.

I looked at Colin as tension built in my shoulders. "Stay here with Caitlyn. Protect her."

"Aye, laird, I will." He bowed his head briefly before heading toward the chair in the corner of the room where he could keep an eye on the door and Caitlyn. Unna crawled onto his lap, and he pressed a kiss to the top of her head. The tenderness between them was the only thing that kept me from believing Colin was a danger to everyone around him. Gone was the calm, laid back, easygoing guy I used to know. In his place was a serious, wounded man whose beast was right beneath the surface of his skin.

I headed out of the room, pausing for one last look at Caitlyn from the doorway. She was what I was fighting for. I'd do whatever was necessary to keep her safe. The long walk to the front door put off the encounter with my brother momentarily. When I finally arrived in the entryway, he was standing outside talking with Kerr and a few other werewolves, laughing and having a good time, as if he'd just gone to the shops. How could they buy into his shite when he'd abandoned them?

I stepped out onto the front stairs, and the laughter between them died. Kerr refused to look at me. My brother wore a haughty grin, and the other werewolves' expressions were a mix of shame, as if they'd been caught doing something wrong, and disgust at me being their Alpha.

I schooled my face, pulling every bit of composure I had around me as if it could protect me from the hurt my brother could always spark. It was like a terrible magic trick he could pull out of his hat. *Dinnae let him get to you. Dinnae let him hurt you.* Maybe if I kept chanting that mantra in my head, the words would shield my emotions, but I sincerely doubted it. I wasn't that lucky.

"Dougal, little brother," Ewan said. "So good to see you again." Condescending laughter lit his eyes, like he was having the time of his life at my expense.

"You're early, Ewan." I walked down the steps, closing the distance to the group.

"My plans changed in Oslo." He shrugged, and the humor he'd worn like a mask melted to his usual cold sneer. "But that means I get to spend more time fixing the Pack my little brother broke."

It was all I could do to keep my hands firmly at my sides. Everything in me wanted to launch myself at Ewan and punch his lights out, but I couldn't do that. That would start more shite than I needed.

"It's good of you to think of the Pack after all these years. You left them—and more importantly, your family—when we needed you the most." The words flew out of my mouth before I could think to rein them in, but they came from my heart. I'd wanted to tell him that for years now, and I finally had my chance.

Ewan ran toward me, his fist cocked back as if he'd hit me like in times past, but he stopped himself at the last minute. I didn't even flinch for the arsehole. He looked toward the group he'd been with, who all appeared incredibly on edge, and gave them his best winning smile and smoothed down his shirt. He lowered his voice so only I could hear him. "Be careful of the way you talk to me. You might regret making any more snide comments like that." With that, he walked into the Pack Headquarters, followed by Kerr and the others.

Ewan and Kerr continued their hushed conversation, but I caught a sad look in Kerr's eyes as he glanced back at me.

Unshed tears burned behind my eyes, but I refused to let them fall as I fled back to my bedroom where Caitlyn still lay unconscious. How would I make it through this challenge alive?

15

COLIN

*D*ougal exuded power like a whip when he walked in. He looked so distraught that I almost wondered if Unna and I should leave, but instead I held Unna against my chest as she slumbered, trying to remain as quiet as I could. If Dougal didn't want me to be there, he'd let me know.

He leaned over my sister and brushed strands of hair from her forehead before placing a tender kiss to her lips.

Feelings warred within me at the gentle display. It made me even sadder for Dougal and my sister. As a wereleopard, she should've been waking up sooner than this, right? Then again, after all the trauma her body had suffered, she had a lot to recover from. I'd seen werewolves come back from worse, though, even getting shot in the chest and having their healing assisted by witches. I tried to keep quiet, but it wasn't easy seeing Dougal in so much pain. Strangely enough, I felt the need to comfort the other man, and that desire made me feel more like myself.

Unna moved a little in my lap, her small hand brushing against my chest. Her pale blonde hair slightly hid the unsightly bruise on her face, and my beast stirred a little under the surface of my skin, anger jabbing at me that disloyal wolves had hurt Caitlyn and Unna. I adjusted Unna in my arms and cradled her to my chest as I stood to get a better look at Dougal and talk to him.

"She's going to be okay," I said, walking to the end of the bed. I didn't feel as confident as my words. "It might take her some time to wake up, but my sister is strong."

Dougal kept his gaze focused on Caitlyn. "I wish she was already awake. I could really use her spunky personality to make me feel less like shite." He ran his hands over his face before turning to look at me. "It feels like it's my fault she's even in this mess. To top that off, I will probably have to fight my brother." He looked back at Caitlyn, brushing a strand of hair from her forehead. "Fights are to the death, and while my brother and I have never gotten along, I don't want to kill him."

I didn't even want to imagine what he was going through emotionally with that. Caitlyn and I had never been super close, but we got along. At least before coming back to Scotland. Now I wished I could've been there for her, and understood what she'd gone through when I was younger. She'd mostly been a strange, feline-smelling sister, but I still cared about her. We didn't talk as much as we should have, but I hoped we could work on fixing that problem. "It feels like what happened to her is my fault." I shook my head. "If I'd paid more attention in the restaurant or been more alert, this might have been avoided. Maybe if I hadn't taken off when she was still recovering."

Looking down at Unna made that decision less painful. I didn't even want to imagine life without my mate, now that I'd found her. She touched my beast in ways that built back some of my control. Regardless of what the future might hold after seven years together, I was happy we at least had this time. "Dinnae fash yerself about yer brother. It may or may not come to that." At Dougal's look, the puzzle pieces clicked together in my mind. Something had happened when he'd left the room to greet his brother. Should I ask, or wait until he felt comfortable talking to me about it?

He turned on the bed to face me fully. "I wish that were true, but I'm not certain about it. He's charming, and the way he gets people to side with him, regardless of how little care he's shown them in the past, really astounds me. Breaks my heart. The Pack I took over from my deceased father and tried my best with has turned their backs on me...for what? The lad who ran away as soon as he could, to experience life away from his family." Dougal shook his head and looked down at his hands. "What if I've become no better than he is, dishonoring our father's memory by making a mockery of the Pack?"

"Nae, don't think like that. You're not like your brother. Never have been. He doesn't know what the word responsibility means, and you've been able to bear enough for both of ye." I looked down at Unna as she made cute, soft snores. My lips twitched in amusement before I could catch myself. "You'll be fine in the fight. I remember how weak yer brother was when the younger wolves were made to spar and fight one another to learn how to control our beasts." That comment made me think, and I cocked my head to the side. "Maybe that's why he was skittish to lead the Pack. Maybe he knew he'd never have a chance of defending himself if challenged." I shrugged a shoulder. "It's no excuse for how he's acted, though."

Dougal sighed and started to hunch his shoulders before he caught himself. "Aye. I remember that as well, but he was always my older brother who teased and tormented me. It was hard to see him as anything but an aggressor regardless of his physical strength. He has mental power that makes his presence equally intimidating."

I could kind of relate to that. Caitlyn and I had our different strengths and weaknesses, but growing up as her younger brother, she was a force to be reckoned with. Knowing more about her now, I could see that what she did was for my protection, not to my detriment like Dougal's situation. I owed Caitlyn so much for being the kind of sister she was. She'd sacrificed a lot for me when I was abducted, and I hadn't given it much thought, much less told her how I appreciated her doing that. "Aye. I remember feeling intimidated by Caitlyn at times, but she was more supportive than anything. Came about it from a different place." I let out a sigh.

Dougal looked over at Caitlyn again. "I bet. She can still be pretty intimidating." He gave me a ghost of a smile. "Dinnae tell her I said that, though."

"I promise." I smiled back at him. "It will be all right." I placed Unna in the chair we'd occupied, and she blinked a few times before bringing her knees up to her chest and dozing back off. Goosebumps dotted her arms, and I covered her with a throw blanket. "Ye ken, ye dinnae have to kill him to win the challenge." I sat near the foot of the bed. "During my time with the Southeastern Pack, I saw a challenge declared on the leader. He's an older man, possibly in his fifties, but he's not someone one would want to cross. A young, pretty stupid person challenged him, and instead of the lad getting killed by the Alpha, he ended up being banished. The Alpha gave him the option of if he wanted to live or not. The lad realized he made a mistake, and he accepted banishment over death."

Dougal nodded. "That's interesting. I'll look into it, see if it's ever been done within the Scottish Pack." He held out his hand to me, and we gave each other a hearty shake.

"Thank ye for the encouragement. I hope I'm able to convince my brother that he doesn't need to die. Unfortunately for me, I don't think he's the type to realize he's made a mistake until it's too late." He shook his head and sighed. "Not that I can say I've done any better. If it weren't for me pursuing Caitlyn, the Pack wouldn't be as fractured as it is."

"Nae, you cannae have that kind of attitude. What's done is done. What matters now is what you do going forward. Stand tough, my friend. Dinnae dwell on what happened. The future is in yer power, if ye are half the leader your father was, and I believe you are, mate, then you'll apply every lesson our laird passed down. Ye'll fix things." I'd never been great at giving pep talks, but I hoped I was doing a halfway decent job. If anyone needed one, Dougal did.

"Aye, you're right. I suppose it's time I try talking with him again." Dougal didn't appear to be ecstatic at the prospect, and I didn't blame him. I wouldn't want to be in his shoes right now.

"If ye want, I can come with you. It's almost lunchtime, so he'll likely be around." Approaching Ewan in a private place wouldn't be a good idea. It'd be easier for him to twist what happened. But there were risks in a public confrontation, too. Regardless, Dougal shouldn't be alone through this. He needed to know I had his back.

He glanced back at Caitlyn wistfully, then looked to Unna. "Are you sure it's a good idea to leave them alone, especially after what almost happened on your way here?"

"It won't take long for ye to talk with him. Plus, ye have an impressively sturdy lock on yer door. I noticed it while I was with them before. If you're worried, ye could always have a trustworthy wolf stand guard outside." That last part would probably be a good idea. I sure as hell wasn't confident about someone else being locked in the room with the girls, but it wouldn't hurt to have someone guarding them from the outside.

"Right. Aye. That's what I'll do." Dougal seemed to shake himself and sat up taller, as if feeling awkward about asking for my advice on this. It was a little odd for an Alpha to lean on someone who wasn't his actual second-in-command, but I was probably the only one he could trust. That was pretty sad, seeing as how we didn't have that great of a relationship before this. Caitlyn was the one thing uniting us. "I'll be back soon with someone to watch them. Thanks for the chat. I appreciate it." He gave me a smile, then walked out of the room, locking the door behind him.

I looked between Caitlyn and Unna, not knowing how this would all end. My advice to him had been more optimistic than I felt. His brother, Ewan, had never been very strong as a kid, but things could change. All I knew was I needed to come up with a plan of my own to get the girls away from here if anything happened to Dougal. I didn't want them to die if the Pack thought they were free to do whatever they liked with Dougal dead. Perhaps the doctor and I needed to have another talk soon.

Unna opened her eyes again, blinking at me. She gave a little yawn. "How long was I out of it? I'm kind of hungry." Her pale blonde hair covered parts of her face, and I crossed the distance between us to kneel before her.

"Ye had a good nap, love. I'll bring ye some food soon, I promise. It's not quite time to eat yet." I brushed the hair from her face and placed a gentle kiss to her lips. Her kind eyes warmed my heart and offered me a wee bit of peace. "When I do have to go, promise me you won't fall asleep. If anything happens, you call me immediately, got it?" I tried to keep my tone matter-of-fact.

Unna frowned, concern creasing her forehead. She

started to stand up, but I placed a hand on her shoulder. "Are you expecting something bad to happen again?"

My hand lifted to her face, and I brushed my thumb over her cheek. "Nae, not necessarily, love. I want to be cautious. Besides, something good may happen, like Caitlyn waking up. I'd like to know that, too."

Unna widened her eyes in understanding. "Okay." She wrapped her arms around my neck, and we remained in one another's arms for a few minutes.

Dougal walked back into the bedroom with Hendrie behind him. Hendrie remained in the doorway, looking a little nervous as if we were plotting something nefarious, but when his eyes touched upon Caitlyn laying battered and still on the bed, his expression saddened. He frowned at me.

"Let's go, Colin." Dougal nodded to Unna with a kind smile.

We left to locate and confront Ewan. I tried not to imagine all the ways this could end very, very badly.

16

DOUGAL

*P*lenty of wolves were already sitting in the grand dining hall befitting of a laird while they waited for Mairi to bring around the meal. My stomach grumbled at the thought of eating, but when I saw Ewan sitting in my chair at the head of the table, my appetite soured.

Kerr was shifting in his chair, looking uncomfortable. He didn't seem thrilled to be hearing whatever Ewan was saying. Kerr glanced turned in our direction, and he frowned, almost apologetically.

"Are ye okay?" Colin said beside me. He kept his gaze scanning the room as if expecting threats to come rushing us at any moment.

"Nae, not really, but I feel better knowing you're here too." I kept going, needing to face this threat head-on. Talking with Colin had helped relieve some of the tension inside me. Knowing that I didn't necessarily have to kill my brother for us to make it out of this was good. However, my brother was too arrogant to leave, especially given the haughtiness he'd displayed thus far.

Not enough of the Pack was behind me to truly enforce

banishment, were they? The last thing I wanted was for the Pack to endure a civil war. I needed to browse my father's extensive library to see if I had books on that subject as soon as I could.

"Aye, and hopefully Mairi will bring the food soon." Colin dropped back a few steps then.

"Hopefully," I grumbled under my breath. At least then, if anything bad went down, the majority of the wolves would be distracted by the food instead of an argument that should best be had in private. I hoped. Doubt pressed onto my chest. Was this even a good idea? But I was already here. To turn back now would be a coward's choice.

Kerr leaned closer to say something to the small group, including Ewan, before standing from his chair. He walked in our direction, his big frame towering over us. "Lad, I don't know what yer doing, but are ye sure ye want to do it in front of everyone?" He looked behind me to Colin. "At least ye have the sense to not come alone." He sighed and shook his head, looking tired. "Perhaps ye should head back to yer room, m'laird. The lunch rush will come and go, then ye can come."

I narrowed my eyes at Kerr, and he took a step back and lowered his head like a submissive wolf. "I will not be told what to do or when I can walk around in my own castle. Do ye understand?" My teeth clenched together, and my jaw ached from how hard I was trying to keep myself in control. My power oozed from me like ripples on water. If I didn't get ahold of myself, I'd be showing the Pack how out-of-control I felt.

"Aye, laird. Understood." Without another word, Kerr turned and led the way to my brother. He stood near the wall, apparently to allow me to sit in his chair.

I would only sit on my own. To do otherwise would show weakness, and with the room falling silent, I knew my members were waiting for the explosion about to happen. Instead, I stood beside my chair, waiting for him to move. When he continued talking with the people around him and ignoring me, I did my best not to drag him out of it by the shirt collar and throw him to the ground. "We need to talk, Ewan."

"I'm already talking. Unlike you, I'm not staying cooped up in a tiny room with a feline mistress while the people look around for their Alpha." Ewan laughed a little, but none of the people near us did. They waited with slightly widened, watchful eyes. I could taste their fear on my tongue, and a small part of me appreciated it. At least they knew the danger that lurked nearby, unlike my arrogant, idiotic brother.

I slapped my hands on the table in front of Ewan and enjoyed seeing him jump. I pulled the chair back and slid it a few feet away before he could sit again. "A word, brother."

Ewan looked at the chair and returned his gaze to me, looking shocked that I'd done such a thing. "A word? This is how you ask to speak with me? You should've had your lap dog approach me like a proper Alpha. The only thing you'll be getting from me is…" His voice shook a little before he cleared his throat, then raised his voice. "Is two days from now when you accept my challenge, and we fight!"

The Pack hall went so quiet that even without supernatural hearing, if a pin dropped, everyone would've heard it.

I clenched my jaw. How typical of him to twist things like this. "As ye wish." My brogue thickened with emotion, and I leaned into him so only he heard my next words. "I was going to give ye a chance to leave before things got bloody, but it seems like you're enjoying being the center of attention. Think of the challenges ye will receive when the Pack realizes who you *really* are." I leaned back a little, and a sarcastic smile spread across my lips. My beast growled his approval. If I didn't get out of the hall, I wasn't sure how the scene would change, and I couldn't afford to strike my brother in public. It would cause more harm than it was worth.

Suddenly, Mairi and a couple of the Pack members helping her came bustling in with the meal. She was as upbeat and happy as ever, but she looked over at us as if she could sense how wrong things were. She called out in a cheery voice, trying to calm the situation, "Food's here, lads. Come get it while it's hot." Then she headed to a small side table, and they set up the food for the wolves to make their own plates.

Colin walked up to stand at my side. "That didn't go so well."

I glanced over at him with an eyebrow lifted. "You don't say. So much for trying to talk sense into him. Now he's scheduled a date for the challenge." Part of me was strangely relieved that there was a firm date when everything would be over one way or another. The more reasonable part knew that things being over could mean my death, my brother's death...and worse yet, Caitlyn's death, too. My stomach soured to the point of nausea.

Once the wolves were out of our range, I turned to look at Colin and whispered, "I know you're returning to the United States once this mess clears up. If something happens to me, take Caitlyn with ye. I don't care what she thinks of the idea. Make sure she's okay." I sighed. "Promise me you will, mate."

Colin leveled his gaze, and he nodded. "Aye, I promise. She'll be safe regardless of what happens, but don't give up hope." He placed a hand on my shoulder. "You're stronger than him, and worthy of happiness. Believe in yerself." With that, he let his hand drop and headed off toward the growing food line.

Sure, he was probably right. Optimism was never my strong suit when it came to conflict with my brother. But Colin cared about this situation, too, because his sister's life was at stake. Perhaps I should trust what he said.

I watched the wolves move through the food line and settle down at the table once they'd filled their plates. Ewan started to come back toward the end of the table, but he saw me still standing there and made a U-turn, heading off to some other spot to eat. I gritted my teeth, but this could be for the best.

If only we didn't have to be enemies. I wished he could be a caring brother. It wasn't as if I had any other living family I could count on. The world closed in on me, and I felt so alone. The one light in my life was unconscious. I needed her to wake up if I had any chance of maintaining my composure and getting through this.

Colin came through the line with two plates. At first, I thought he was bringing me one, but then I remembered Unna. Right. He was taking care of his mate. I went through the line to grab some food as well. The chances of Caitlyn being awake was unlikely. I was pretty sure Unna or Hendrie would have found us and shared the news. I'd made that clear to Hendrie when I asked him to stand guard.

I met up with Colin, and we headed back to my room. The thought of missing out on a meal with the Pack didn't affect me as much this time. Some of them had already made their poor decision. If they thought they wanted my brother to lead them, then they would see how much of a coward he was if—or when—his reign began.

Everything depended on how the challenge in two days went. Even though Colin had tried to encourage me, I still was skeptical about my chances. All I could remember from our childhood was Ewan beating me down. I'd never experienced him as a weaker opponent, the way Colin had during Pack sparring. Then again, he didn't have to deal with the verbal and emotional abuse from Ewan like I did.

I nodded to Hendrie who stood by the door, and he took a step to the side. "Do you still need me here, laird? I'd be happy to stay." He bowed his head.

"Nae, Hendrie, I think we'll be all right now. Grab yourself some lunch before it's all gone." I walked to the door and unlocked it using my key. My bed chambers were my private sanctuary, aside from my study, and I fiercely guarded my privacy.

When we stepped inside, Unna was watching television while Caitlyn lay in the same position as before. Her body was completely still, aside from her breathing. My heart ached to see her open her eyes, to be kissed by her, to talk with her again. Not being able to share my life with my mate would be a fate worse than death.

Roy would come by later to check on her again. Maybe I could ask him when he estimated she would wake up. He might know better now how quickly she was healing. Hell, I had no idea. I just wanted her to be alive and safe.

Colin handed over a plate of food to Unna, and she sat up straighter in the chair. They seemed such like opposites: she was cute and naïve, while Colin was gruff and jaded. I didn't know how they made it work, but apparently they were good together, each providing something the other person needed. He seemed to relax around her and almost become the guy he was before his kidnapping. He'd been such an easygoing lad then, as opposed to the man who'd returned just under a week ago. That guy was almost unrecognizable to me.

Colin sat on the floor beside the chair, letting Unna remain comfortable.

I perched on the bed beside her, propping my plate on one leg. The television droned in the background, and I ate quietly with the others, watching the telly. My thoughts drifted for a while as I stared at the news.

Before long, Colin and Unna went off to the bedroom they would stay in a few doors down the hallway. Strength in numbers. If there was any trouble, we'd be able to quickly reach one another. I stripped off my clothes and showered before pulling on some sweatpants and falling asleep beside Caitlyn. It had been a long day, and I suspected more of those would be in my future.

17

CAITLYN

*B*lackness enveloped me in its cool embrace, and I was floating along on a lazy river. My leopard stalked the water's edge, roaring at me to wake up, but her cries didn't matter right now. The only thing that mattered was letting the slow currents carry me away.

A splash drew my attention toward the leopard who was now swimming toward me. My heart rate sped a little, and I tried to use my arms to paddle away, but the only thing I could do was lay in the dark water. Drawing closer, my leopard clamped her teeth around my shoulder, careful not to bite down too hard. Her touch arced between us like electricity, and the renewed connection made me gasp and flail my arms.

I plunged under the water, but the leopard wouldn't let go. She dragged me back to the surface and swam me to shore, pulling me out of the darkness.

Pain flooded my entire body, and my eyes shot open to a darkened room, only the faint glow of a night-light cast enough light for me to see. I groaned softly and tried to sit up, but everything I did shot waves of agony through me.

The familiar warmth of another body lay to my right, and my breath caught in my throat to see Dougal with his eyes closed, taking deep, steady breaths. He looked different from when I'd last seen him, a little haggard, with lines at the corners of his lips and eyes as if from too much frowning.

I lifted my hand, ignoring how much it hurt, and brushed my fingers over the stubble lining his jaw. I drew his scent into my lungs, and it soothed me, making me want to shift closer to him and lose myself in his arms. As I started to put that plan into motion, he turned his face into my hand, then froze.

Dougal cracked his eyes open slowly as if expecting an assault. He jerked upright and scanned the room, then his gaze descended upon me. His mouth dropped open, and he stared at me as if unsure what to say.

"Hello, my love," I said, my voice cracking a little. My throat hurt, and I placed my hand to my neck, feeling more pain as I touched the skin.

"Caitlyn, you're awake." His breath came out in harsh pants, and he leaned down to brush a kiss to my lips. "God, I missed ye so bloody much. I…I was very worried about ye. I'll have the Pack doctor come at once—"

"*Och*, nae, I'll be okay. I've gotten through the worst of it. Tell me what's going on." I trailed my finger over his lower lip. "Why are ye looking so worn out? What did I miss?"

Uncertainty filled his features, and he pulled away a little. Did he think that because I'd been injured, I couldn't handle whatever had gone on while I was unconscious? That look hurt worse than my injuries.

"For fuck's sake, Dougal. Stop trying to treat me like porcelain. I'm not as fragile as I look. Ye should bloody well ken that by now." I dropped my hand back to my side, feeling the sting of hurt course through my chest.

"Love, I know ye aren't porcelain. You've been through so

much. I only hoped to have more time to revel in you being conscious before ye hit me with these questions." He carefully ran his hand over my hair, brushing it from my face. "However, it's not safe or fair not to let you know." He met my gaze, and it looked like it took effort for him, which wasn't like the tough Alpha who nearly ravished me in the cage downstairs. "My brother arrived shortly after you did." He cleared his throat. "Tomorrow is the challenge. The day I've been dreading. I know ye might not like the idea, but I'm going to have Colin take you and his mate away today. If I don't..." He drew in a breath. "If Ewan wins, I don't want you to be hurt."

My world shook, and if I hadn't been lying down, I might've fallen over. How was I supposed to react to that? Did Dougal really think our plight was hopeless? Nae, I couldn't take off with my brother and leave him.

"How can ye even suggest that?" I said, my voice breaking a little. "I cannae go while yer facing yer brother. We're mated. I need to be here for ye. Nae, I cannae go. "

Dougal clenched his hands into fists and pressed them against his forehead, looking like he was about to explode. "Lass, I love ye more than you'll ever know. If you are here, and if something happens to me, or if ye were hurt again—or worse, killed—I would never forgive myself. I need to know you're safe so I can focus on the task at hand." He dropped his hands and sighed. His expression told me that he expected my full cooperation, but I couldn't stand by and let him face this alone. While I admitted my being stubborn about the funeral might have been a mistake, in this I would remain resolute.

"Sorry, love. I care too much for ye to let you go through this alone. You'll need to find a different way of putting aside your worries." I placed my hand over one of his. "I have faith in ye, and in Colin. While I might not be at my best, I know I won't come to any harm with the two of ye around. "

His expression soured a little, but he gently pressed his forehead to mine. "You have a special way of not making things easy for me, love. Perhaps a bit too much faith in my abilities as well. I only hope ye ken something I don't. If you were killed, I don't know what I'd do."

I placed my hand against the back of his neck, feeling the tightly bunched muscles. "I dinnae have too much faith. I have the right amount." I tilted my head up a little to press a kiss against his lips, despite the pain. His soft lips on mine drove every other sensation away. My life felt whole again when he was near. How did I ever think being away from him would make my life better, when I wanted so desperately to stay with him now?

Dougal cupped my face with both of his hands and deepened the kiss between us. "How did I come to deserve such a wonderful mate as ye?" His tongue stroked mine, and heat flooded my body as my nerve endings came alive. He dropped his hand toward my throat, and the movement broke the intimacy between us as pain shot through my neck.

I cried out, pushing at his firm chest. The memory of George looming over me in the restroom with his hand on my throat startled me. My heart raced in my chest, and I trembled, despite the warm blankets covering me.

Dougal jerked away like I'd burned him. "Caitlyn, I'm so sorry." He reached for me as if wanting to hold me, but then dropped his hands. "Forgive me, love. I didn't mean to hurt you." His hands balled into fists in his lap, and he turned away from me on the bed. I couldn't see his face anymore, but his torso was nearly vibrating with emotion.

Silence stretched between us, and I drew the blankets toward my chin, not wanting to feel so vulnerable again. Not in front of him or anyone. I'd thought that seeing Alistair put in the ground would help with the fears and nightmares I'd had, but ever since coming to the Scottish Pack's HQ, I learned there were many others out there like him. Perhaps I'd never truly be free from that pain.

"I failed you. I promised I'd make sure you were never hurt again, but I...I failed. Who did all of this to you?" He turned back to face me. A single tear spilled down his cheek. I'd never seen him show emotions like this. Alphas didn't do that kind of thing. They were strong, stoic. At least that's what I'd thought up until this point.

I fought against the pain that kept me lying flat on the bed, digging my nails into the bedspread and using my strength to help move my screaming muscles. "Dougal, this wasn't your fault." I ran my thumb over his cheek, wiping away the moisture. "Dinnae ever feel like it was. The only ones to blame are the wolves who did this."

Flashes of their faces threaded through my head. "I... One of them was named George. The jerk at the funeral who I fought before you pulled me off of him. The other man was an arrogant, cocky arsehole. I'm not sure what his name was, but I know he had greying hair. He wasn't as tall as George." I couldn't remember much more detail about him.

Dougal's face reddened, and he raised his chin a little, looking a little defiant. "I think I know who you're talking about. Damn it all." He ran his tongue over his lower lip. "I thought I could trust her. She betrayed me. I should have known the minute I knew Colin told me you were injured. I was just too fucking blind to see it." His brogue thickened, and he gently pulled me closer. "I'll make it right."

My mouth dropped open. He knew who did this? My heart sunk in my chest, but why was he talking about a female? Neither of the attackers had been female. What did he mean? I didn't realize I'd asked that last part until he replied.

"The night you left, I went to the wake for Duncan and Alistair. Things were rough, and you were gone. I was upset, so I talked with Mairi. She was curious about if you would be attending it too." He let out a sigh. "I told her you'd left. Little did I know she'd pass that information on to her brother and her ex-husband."

I cocked my head to the side. "Ex-husband? I thought wolves mated for life?"

Dougal snorted. "Sometimes wolves get it wrong. We're not perfect either. Mates are looked upon as some sort of supernatural bond, but not all see it that way. The beasts might be drawn to one another, but the human sides of our nature might not necessarily agree. You've met George—not exactly Mr. Perfect material, aye?"

My eyes widened, and I opened my mouth to say something. What was there to say about that, though? Any anger I'd felt toward the woman almost edged toward pity... almost. Instead, I opted to shake my head. "Aye, he's not at all."

"I'll deal with them, and I'll see who else Mairi has in on this. The Pack won't be thrilled with her being barred from the kitchen, but it's better to be safe right now." He wrapped his arms around me gently, then put me at arm's length. "We'll sort this out." He sounded more hopeful than he'd been in a while. Knowing who was behind the attacks might not be a lot, but I could relate to his optimism. At least some step could be taken toward making things right and getting the Pack sorted again.

Dougal helped me lay back on the bed again, and we cuddled—as well as could be expected with my healing injuries—there until the sun peeked beneath the blackout curtains.

We must have dozed off at some point, because a sudden knock made me try to bolt upright, although my body once again refused to cooperate. I choked on a scream and lay back down.

Dougal stared down at me with concern etching lines in his forehead. "Are you okay, love?"

I pointed my index finger and croaked out, "Door."

He lifted his lips in frustration but rose from the bed as another set of hard knocks reverberated through the large room. Each time the person pounded on it, my head throbbed in time with the bangs.

Colin stood in the doorway when Dougal opened the door. His fist was in the air, about to continue knocking. At his side, Unna tugged at Colin's sleeve. They both glanced in my direction, and the look on Colin's face was like sunshine breaking through rain clouds. His whole face brightened, and he tried to push past Dougal, except Dougal wasn't feeling as friendly now after all the knocking.

"Colin," I said with a smile. "Good morning, ye arse. Let them in, my love."

Dougal took a step to the side. His expression brightened the barest amount, and he glanced into the hallway as if surprised. "Hendrie? What the hell are ye doing here?"

Hendrie peeked into the room and lifted his hand in a wave. "Doing my duty. Keeping watch over you and your lady, m'laird."

Colin clapped Dougal on the back. "Now's not the time or place, laird. Just let Hendrie continue his watch."

Dougal nodded his head, gave Hendrie a brief smile, and closed the door. Something like awe flickered over Dougal's face. Perhaps he had more supporters than we'd first thought. "Maybe it's a good thing he's there. Caitlyn helped me pinpoint her attackers. I know who did this to her."

DOUGAL

oday was the day. I tried to focus on the conversation I'd had with Colin about the fight, and how the new Pack he was in banished one of their wolves. That had never been done within our Pack, to my knowledge. The books in the study didn't appear to have any information on it either, aside from the rare cases when a wolf wasn't fit to run with the Scottish Pack, and he was banished for whatever reason. But none of those men were challengers to the Pack's Alpha. I paced in the study, not prepared to see anyone, not even Caitlyn.

I hated leaving her in the bedroom with her brother and Unna as company, but I had to collect my thoughts before I could see her, possibly to say 'goodbye,' depending on how the fight went.

If she were in better shape, I would've made love to her in all the positions I could think of, but with all the trauma her body suffered, it was better to wait... I hoped there was something to wait for. The pain she'd been in when we were only kissing hurt to witness.

Books were spread out in piles on the floor, where I'd

been sitting and skimming through them. I ran my hands through my hair, feeling the urge to pull it out, but I dropped my hands to my side. If I was going to die, I didn't want them to bury a corpse with chunks of hair missing.

I leaned back against my desk. I knew there was no point in me stressing myself in here. The challenge was this afternoon, and I needed not to run away from the one I loved most. I needed to spend time with her, in case today was our last day together.

Those thoughts weren't the kind I should be having. I should be more confident in how the fight would go, but I couldn't let myself hope. If things didn't go well, I needed to have a plan, not wishful thinking.

I scooped up the books from the floor and placed them on one of the chairs facing the desk, so they wouldn't be stepped on and messed up. Then I headed out, locking the door behind me. I walked directly toward my bedroom, and opened the door to see Caitlyn smiling with Colin and Unna. They were laughing at something, and my dark mood made me feel like I'd interrupted.

I forced a smile onto my face and closed the door. Colin's grin died a little when he saw me, and part of me wished I'd stayed in the study. Then Caitlyn lifted her arm toward me.

"Dougal! Where have ye been? I woke up to find Colin and Unna staring at me as they cuddled in that chair." She maintained her smile, and it warmed my heart a little.

"I went off to the study to research a few things." I wondered what they'd talked about, especially since we all knew today was the challenge. I looked at Colin as if he'd give me some kind of sign, but his face remained a little closed off.

Colin nudged Unna from his lap. "Let's go fetch Caitlyn some breakfast. I'm sure the lass is famished after all of her time unconscious."

Unna nodded and gave us a cheery wave. "We'll be back."

I nodded back to her, still amazed at the fact Colin found someone like that. The fact he'd protected her from humans without giving into his beast, and he trusted his wolf around her now, also impressed me. He really was pulling himself back from the ledge he'd been on when he came back to Scotland.

I crossed the distance to Caitlyn and took her hand. "Hello, love." I pressed a kiss to her hand and smiled at her. This time it wasn't a strain to do so. It was natural, because I was happy to be with her, even if I knew our time together might be short-lived.

"Hi." Caitlyn pulled me closer and kissed me on the lips gently. "I've missed you." She looked at me from mere inches away, and something changed in her gaze. "*Och*, I know something's going on. Colin wouldn't really say anything, and you've been off since I woke up. What's wrong?"

I started to back away a little, but Caitlyn kept her hand on me. While I could've easily broken free from her grip, I didn't want to hurt her, either physically or emotionally. I sighed. "Today is the challenge. I'm not thrilled with the prospect of fighting my brother. Colin told me something about his new Pack banishing someone who challenged an Alpha." I sighed. "I was hoping for some option like that."

The smile on her lips died, but she didn't shove me away like I thought she might. In fact, she pulled me close again. "Nae, it can't be challenge day. I've only just come back to consciousness. I...I dinnae want to lose you when I've only found you again." She looked me in the eyes, beseeching me. "Cannae we just take off? Go somewhere no one will find us?"

I frowned. The thought had occurred to me earlier too, but my duty to the Pack—and my desire not to be a coward like my brother—prevented me. I didn't want to die, but I would be a rogue wolf if I fled a challenge, and that would be no life for either me or Caitlyn. "I'm sorry, love. It's not that simple. I'm not happy about this challenge, but I can't turn my back on werewolf tradition. If I were to run away with you, we'd always have to look over our shoulders. That's not a life to live."

"Aye, I know." Caitlyn's face fell. From what she'd told me, I had a feeling she knew about that kind of life all too well from when she'd been trying to rescue Colin. She knew what I'd said was true. We couldn't just run and try to do this the easy way.

"Aye, you do, love. That's why I want you to be safe and leave before the challenge starts. I don't want there to be a chance of the Pack killing you if I lose. Right now you're not able to protect yourself." I cupped the back of her neck and pressed my lips against hers again, then gently touched our foreheads together. "I need to know you're safe if I'm going to be able to do this."

Caitlyn pushed against my chest and shook her head. "Nae, I'm not okay with that. Like I said before, I might not be in the best shape, but I refuse to leave your side. I want to be there and watch the challenge like everyone else." Her frown intensified. "I won't take no for an answer."

I knew exactly how well she took no for an answer. Maybe if I'd given in and shown the Pack who was boss with the funeral situation, some of this mess could have been avoided. If I'd kept her closer, I might have protected her. If I'd not given so many fucks about the Pack over my mate, she would be whole, and I wouldn't feel so weak right now.

"Aye, I ken ye won't. I also know what will probably happen if I were to tell you no. Instead, I guess I'll need to come up with a plan on how to fight *and* keep ye safe if something were to happen to me. I know my brother. He doesn't care about anyone but himself. If the Pack wants ye to die, if he were to gain power he'd have no qualms about giving in to their demands." I gently trailed my knuckles over Caitlyn's cheek. "You're precious. I can't have you hurt."

She smiled at me and leaned into my hand. "I feel the same way about ye, and I have faith in ye that you'll win. Yer brother isn't the courageous, strong man that ye are. Ye have what it takes to win and protect me yourself."

The amount of belief she had in me both scared and thrilled me. "Thanks, love. I don't know if I deserve all of that faith, but I appreciate it nonetheless." The fact she believed in me almost helped me to believe in myself. Now I'd need to scrounge up the few Pack members I trusted to put a plan into place, making sure that Caitlyn was taken care of regardless of what happened during the challenge.

"You're welcome. Ye do deserve my faith. Ye also deserved your Pack's confidence, but that'll soon take care of itself." She yawned, and her eyes drifted shut as a knock on the door disrupted the moment.

"Who is it?" I called out.

The door opened a crack. "It's Colin. We brought breakfast." He waited a moment before opening the door further, as if afraid to find us having sex. When he was certain we were decent, he opened the door wider and let Unna pop inside before him. Each of them carried two plates, and Colin pushed one of them my way. "It's best if ye keep up yer strength. You'll need it for later," he whispered. But this close, we both knew Caitlyn could hear what was being said. She had sensitive hearing, too.

"She knows about today." I waited to take the plate, carefully helping Caitlyn into a sitting position and propping the generous amount of pillows behind her. She grimaced and made a couple of painful sounds as I got her settled, but finally, she was in a good spot to eat what Unna offered.

"Aye, I do." Caitlyn frowned at Colin, and he scowled back at her.

"It wasnae my news to tell. Besides, I wasnae sure if he'd talked to ye about that yet or not." Colin sighed. "Ye were in such a good mood, and I didn't want to spoil it." He shrugged. "Guess it didn't matter after all."

"It's fine, mate. Caitlyn and I talked it over. Instead of listening to reason and leaving, she wants to remain here while the challenge takes place." I looked between Colin and Caitlyn, who were now almost glowering at one another. It was suddenly very easy to tell that they were siblings.

"Bloody hell. The shite you will," Colin said as he paced the room while chomping on a piece of bacon. "Ye shouldn't be anywhere near here. If anything happens, they will kill you, sis. I don't want either ye or Unna to be hurt by the loons in the Pack." He broke his stare at Caitlyn to look at his mate, Unna, who was frowning at him.

"Colin, if she wants to stay with him, that's not your choice to make. If I were in her place, I would do the same thing. It's not your decision, it's hers." Unna sat in the chair and scooped some scrambled eggs onto her fork, eating calmly as if the rest of the room wasn't as high strung as they were. She was like a voice of reason.

"Nae, and it's not your say either, Unna. I need to keep ye safe, too. I promised yer pa I would. I can't keep you and my sis safe against a whole Pack of werewolves. That's too much for me." He shook his head. "Nae." The energy in the room became intense, and I could tell that he was feeling his beast overwhelm him again.

I set my plate on the nightstand beside me and crossed the bedroom toward him, taking him by the arm to get his attention. He glanced at my arm, and then looked me in the eyes as if to say something, but I sent a wave of power into him. "Calm down, Colin. You're not in a good head space here. Ye told me yourself that the challenge could be won. Don't fall back on me now." He let out a breath as his beast inched back from the surface, intimidated by my own. "We'll come up with a plan to keep them safe. We'll have more wolves than ye looking after them, and I'll arrange an easy getaway just in case. Understand?"

He nodded. He still looked uneasy, but he relaxed a wee bit, at least.

God help me if the one person I trusted with Caitlyn's life, and who'd encouraged me before, was having this much anxiety about the fight. Was I doomed to die?

DOUGAL

*T*he cool breeze carried with it a distant promise of warmer times to come, but I could only smell the cold and the gathering moisture in the air. The wolf within me grew restless as it caught the scent of my brother, who was watching me from the other side of the clearing. He cracked his knuckles as the Pack surrounded us, waiting for the battle to begin.

Colin and Unna, along with Roy, Hendrie, and a few others, stood to one side with Caitlyn, who sat in a lawn chair. They were a little away from everyone else. Caitlyn's presence made me nervous, but she'd been adamant. The idea of her watching my potential death distressed me. What would happen to her if I lost? Would the Pack kill her soon after? I only hoped that Colin and the few wolves I trusted would be able to whisk the lasses to safety if that happened.

I took a deep breath, letting the smell of pine trees and home help calm me. The birds sang, and small animals scurried within the woods. As if today was like any other day before it. Another day in the house I'd grown up in. Safe, warm, and familiar.

The trick worked until I saw the smug grin on my brother's face. He looked confident, like he knew beyond a shadow of a doubt that he would win. He'd win, and he would gladly end me. That look almost unraveled me. How could my brother act that way? So cold and uncaring about his family? I'd never been able to understand him, and it appeared that wasn't going to change anytime soon.

Kerr came toward the two of us. As the official second-in-command of the Pack, he would officiate this, even if I didn't trust him as far as I could throw him. He'd betrayed me, and I wasn't sure I'd ever be able to let that slide. However, I had to believe he had enough scruples to ensure neither of us entered the ring with any advantages. Neither silver nor wolf's magic were allowed. While honor usually assured that whoever entered the duel would do so with tradition in mind, I wasn't sure if that applied to my brother. Therefore, Kerr took his time before declaring us both able to fight.

We both were shirtless and dressed only in exercise shorts. Steam slowly rose from our bodies in the cool air. Kerr examined each of us in turn, ruffling our hair and ensuring neither had any needle marks to indicate cheating through chemical enhancement. After a few moments, he nodded.

"The Alpha and his challenger are ready," Kerr said, his voice booming over the gathered crowd.

"Fur or fists, brother?" I asked, barely keeping the building growl from drowning out my actual words. The effect on my brother was fleeting but immediate. For the briefest moment, his pupils dilated, switching from those a predator rising to the challenge, to those of prey. It wasn't much, nor would it likely be something he'd graciously admit, but it gave me something to cling to. Even though he acted brave, he was just as nervous about this as I was.

"We'll start with fists. Fighting as beasts is rather barbaric, isn't it?" He sneered at me. His arrogant attitude grated on my nerves, but I forced myself to play things cool. The first one to lose focus would be easy prey. His desire to cling to his human skin stirred curiosity in me. It was a slight toward tradition, and his behavior toward the duel gave me confidence that the Pack needed me to fight for them, as well as for myself and my mate. Still, if he hadn't been my brother, this would've been easier.

"Fists it is, Kerr." I bit down on the negative grumbling that came unbidden into my mind. The beast wanted to goad Ewan, get him riled up and agitated. I soothed my wolf. A laird didn't need tricks. A laird set an example, and the Pack followed. Something my brother had always failed to see.

"Both men are ready. They are without magic, of which I sensed none. They are free of silver, of which I found none. The fight for our Pack begins now!" Kerr yelled and strode back toward the crowd. His task was mostly done. Now he watched the fight until one or the other of us died.

I tilted my head to the side, keeping my eyes focused on my brother as we circled each other. It didn't take long for him to become unnerved, and he mirrored my movements. We'd gone a quarter of a circle, and I kept a careful watch on both his eyes and his feet. Up and down. Up and down. His gaze darted between my eyes and arms, as if expecting an attack any minute now. Up...down, up...down, up... I lunged forward fast, letting adrenaline carry me forward.

My brother came forward at once, throwing a quick right jab. His punch came up short, and I grabbed his outstretched arm, pulling it past me. I grinned at him and leaned backward, driving my knee into his oncoming momentum. His chin struck my leg, but to his credit, he threw himself further into his lunge, barely scraping against me. His left leg caught my shoulder painfully, but by then it had been robbed of its force.

My wolf bared his fangs as I swept my legs out and caught Ewan's ankle, driving him off balance. The advantage didn't last, but it gave me an opportunity to throw an off-handed jab once I was back on my feet. It connected with his chest. To a human, the impact might've been a severe blow, but to my kin, it wasn't as much of a threat.

Bloody hell. To shite with this. I edged closer to him, but that was a mistake.

Apparently, he'd pulled his punches before. He staggered against my blow, as if on purpose. The moment I closed in, a grin spread across his face. I shifted my weight to try to avoid his haymaker punch that came out of nowhere. His fist scraped my cheek and jaw, barely missing my eye. Had that connected fully, I might've lost my right eye. The thought struck a nerve in my bestial side like a hammer. A blinded wolf was a useless one. What drew me back, though, was the smug smile on his face.

Everything slowed down. As I turned against the momentum of his blow, I grabbed his outstretched arm before it drew back and bit down. Even in human form, I had enough force behind my bite to cause damage. Unlike a human, I didn't care if my teeth were pulled out or even torn off. I'd grow new ones. Pain ached in my jaw as my brother jerked his arm away while my teeth were embedded in his flesh, but I could only imagine his.

Blinded by reaction and not by thought, he held his hand against his chest. The coward never had been one for down-and-dirty fighting before, and it showed. Blood coated the inside of my mouth, and I realized that in the process of Ewan pulling his arm back, he'd torn a gaping wound in it, as well as taking one of my teeth.

Instinctively, I ran my tongue over my teeth and found

that the missing one had come from my lower jaw. "*Och.* Come on, brother. Is that the best ye have? Can't you handle the pain?" I asked, spitting our blood onto the ground between us.

"Oh, you'll know pain," Ewan muttered, pulling back from me. He took three steps back, and I followed aggressively, feeling a bit overzealous after the bite. He did a spinning kick that hit me on the thigh before moving away again. The kick hurt, but the muscle was intact. He hadn't leaned into it enough to cause damage that I'd need to worry about.

Memories of my past, my father, and my upbringing came unbidden into my mind as I waded through the several hard and powerful blows that followed the kick. He landed a few strong ones, but so did I. And he kept stepping toward the forest. I would catch the coward soon enough.

He tried another of his fake openings, and I took a single step forward, waiting for his move. He curled his toes and pulled his hips back. *When had he learned martial arts?* I thought before his left hand moved in for a cheap shot.

I'd been so focused on his legs, I hadn't noticed his hand until he was already halfway into the move. Unavoidably, his palm would hit. What I could control now was how to take the impact. I swallowed hard, closed my eyes, and pressed my chin to my chest.

His palm connected with my face, where my Adam's apple had been a fraction of a second ago. Instead of a broken windpipe, I gained a solid punch to my jaw, and a headache that took half my field of vision from me. My brother had put a lot of momentum into the hit. Instead of fighting it, I rode the impact and went limp. My legs rose upward, and I tucked my head. Without thinking, I moved my left arm behind my head, letting it take the impact. *Fuck.*

A loud snap sounded as my hand broke in a few places,

but my skull remained intact. The moment my hips hit the grass, I rolled to the right and kicked into his left knee. Not waiting to see the results, I rolled a few more times, then rose to my feet. My left arm hung useless at my side. My vision was blurred, and blood and saliva dripped from my split lip.

"I'll only ask you twice. Yield if you want to live, brother," I shouted the words as he climbed to his feet. For a moment I hoped he would, then he laughed.

"You bloody fool. You are nothing. You are so beneath me, it's not even funny." Ewan smirked at me and moved his fists back into a fighting pose.

Would I have to kill him?

I rose to my full height and struck him with a series of jabs that I intentionally left short, followed by a step closer on my left side, then an uppercut. He was so busy, and so confident he'd stay a step ahead of me, that he didn't see my right arm move until it was too late. His jaw met the uppercut, and it sent him reeling. Something about it felt off, though. When the impact hit him, he didn't bother to step away. Instead, he'd leaned in closer after it landed.

My wolf's instincts kicked in, and I leapt to the right. It was too late, though. I smelled my blood in the air. As I landed, I became painfully aware of the growing red slice in my torso. The all too familiar burn of a silver wound came even before I saw the small silver knife in his hand. The sharpened blade had likely been buried in the field's grass before the match. Its poor quality had left enough of an uneven surface for grass to stick to.

"You are mine now, brother. Even your pathetic brain must realize this is over now. I have silver. We're far enough away from Kerr, and no one can interfere in this match. I shall cut you open." He sneered at me and stalked closer. Technically, he was right. He hadn't had the knife at the beginning. He'd swear he was following the rules. To stop the duel would mean losing my honor, and my life.

Blood slowly trickled from me as I made a few more tries to get closer to Ewan. A fresh set of scratches from the silver blade rewarded each attempt. Each little nick was painful on its own, but together, it felt like my arm was on fire. "It's already over, brother. If you yield, I'll let you lick my boots each time I walk over your lass's grave. There's no place for her here," he said with a hateful gleam in his eye as he nodded toward Caitlyn.

"Ye are many things, but you're not smart. Never threaten a wolf's mate." I snarled, feeling pure unadulterated hatred toward him. If he even made a wrong move toward Caitlyn, I would kill him. *Think. I need to think.*

Ewan took a few steps closer, and I moved out of the way. I needed to decipher a pattern, something I could use to get close and end him before this became too difficult. "Useless now, aren't you? With your broken arm and your bleeding wounds, you look like a beast that needs to be put down."

Something clicked in my head, and it took all my control to keep a neutral expression on my face. *Aye, let the arse think my arm is useless.* It might be painful, but I was able to torture my muscles to move. It'd cause more problems, and a lot of pain, but I had a way.

When he took another step forward and ran his mouth again, I jabbed him in the face and was rewarded by the sharp sting of silver. "You just don't," my brother began to say as I took another two swings at him, each one giving me the same piercing pain, "learn, do you?" This time, I made my move. Agony shot through my left arm as I slammed it into the knife. A bone crunched inside my arm, pushing through the muscle and poking through the skin into the cool air.

"Don't talk shite about my mate," I growled as I twisted his right arm, breaking his wrist as I slammed my head against his in a hard headbutt. The impact made my ears ring. My body screamed in agony, my spirit was nearly spent, and the knife was lodged in my arm. His wrist dangled from his hand at an odd angle, and he whimpered at the sight as I tore the blade from my arm in front of him.

"Do ye understand?" I kicked him backward almost two feet. The wrenching coughs he gave told me he likely had a few broken ribs, but he was still dangerous. He started to push himself to his feet, but he dropped back down as I stalked toward him. "Submit to me and accept banishment from the Scottish Pack." I raised my voice so the entire Pack could hear.

I stood over him. My beast wanted to end him for the harm he'd caused, but I stared at him where he lay beneath me. It took a few seconds before my brain registered his cry.

"I accept banishment, my laird. I accept!" Ewan crumpled and put his arms over his head, curling into a ball. He glanced at me after a moment as if realizing his exile began now, and then he jumped to his feet and ran. The revving of a car engine a little while later and the spray of gravel as he sped off soothed my beast completely.

My shoulders drew back, and I turned toward the Pack, who were still gathered around. They stared with a mixture of awe, happiness, and fear on their faces.

"Does anyone else want to feel my wrath and challenge me?" The words came out in a snarl. They dropped to their knees, a few at a time, their heads bowed in submission. All except for Caitlyn, who sat on the lawn chair with worried pride beaming from her face. I strode across the clearing and offered her my hand, helping her stand.

"Y-ye made it. Ye won," she said, her voice quiet. "I love ye so much."

"I love you too." I pulled her up, letting her wrap her legs around my waist as I supported her backside with my uninjured arm. It wasn't easy with how badly my body hurt, but I needed her close. My gaze drifted over the Pack, then I looked to my fervent supporters. "Lock away Mairi, her brother Tamhas, George…and Kerr. We'll figure out who else needs to be taught their place in time."

Colin nodded. "Aye, laird." Hendrie walked with him as they approached the four of them.

Roy and Unna followed me as I carried Caitlyn back into the castle, toward my bedroom. After the fight, all I wanted was to have my wounds patched and to relax beside Caitlyn. The fact I'd survived felt almost too good to be true, but it gave me a second chance to be the mate Caitlyn deserved. A chance I refused to squander.

CAITLYN

A few days had passed since Dougal and Ewan fought. Even if Dougal hadn't convinced Ewan to accept banishment, Kerr had ruled that Ewan cheated by planting a silver knife by the edge of the clearing. Proceedings had also begun on Mairi, George, and Tamhas. Kerr had been scolded severely and stripped of his high rank in the Pack.

The Pack had warmed to me considerably, much to my surprise. Even Roy, the doctor, treated me with acceptance. Hendrie would replace Kerr as second-in-command once Colin returned to the United States and the Southeastern Pack. I dreaded seeing him—and even Unna—leave, but at least we were only a phone call away.

I stood on the porch at the top of the stairs as Gordon packed the few bags Colin and Unna had in the boot of the black car. He waited beside the back door patiently as the two of them strode back toward me.

"I'll miss ye, sis. I wish we could've spent a wee bit more time together while I was here, but ye are always welcome to stay with us if ye two come visit." Colin gently hugged me before stepping back, naturally being careful of my still-healing injuries. He would be a perfect mate for Unna.

"Thanks. So long as ye dinnae make me sleep in the car again from the noise." I cracked a smile at the memory.

Unna dipped her head and blushed. She chewed her lower lip and looked up at me. "We don't know each other well, but I promise I'll look after your brother." She hugged me too.

"It makes me happy to ken someone will be around to take care of him. You two are good for one another." I patted her softly on the back, feeling emotions tighten my throat. If I didn't get them under control, I'd end up crying in front of everyone. That was the last thing I wanted to do. I pulled away from her and looked to my left.

Dougal wrapped his arm around my shoulder. He leaned in and brushed a kiss against my temple. "There, there, love. I'm sure they'll come for the occasional visit."

Colin nodded. "Aye, I don't want to repeat past mistakes. I dinnae want to imagine being without a home and family again. I'll ring ye when we arrive." He flashed me a genuine smile, and for a brief moment, I saw true happiness in my younger brother again. He started to turn around, but then stopped and held a hand out to Dougal. "Thank ye for being good to my sister. She's in good hands with you."

Dougal pulled him in for a manly hug instead, and I bit back my laughter. "The pleasure is all mine." He winked at me, and heat warmed my insides. "I'll send word to the Southeastern Pack's Alpha that ye are on your way back. Safe travels to ye both." He smiled at Unna and waved.

"Thank you," Unna said, beaming as she waved back before descending the stairs, walking hand-in-hand with Colin.

Seeing Colin leave was almost too much for me to handle,

but I'd spent nearly a week with him. I'd never forget that time.

Gordon opened the back passenger-side door for them, and they both waved before climbing inside the car. He slid into the driver's, and they drove off down the gravel driveway to the Edinburgh airport.

After a few moments of standing there in silence, Dougal turned me toward him. "Let's get you inside so you don't get too cold out here. I know a fine way to warm you."

My eyebrows rose toward my hairline, and a wicked grin spread across my lips. "Do ye now, darling Alpha?"

Dougal matched my grin, then gave me a look of mock dismay. "I merely meant a soak in our large Jacuzzi tub. Perhaps I could join you. For added body heat, of course."

"*Och*, of course." I turned toward the front door, a shiver of excitement racing down my spine. "What else could you possibly have planned?"

Dougal stopped me from getting too far away. "Many things, love. All of which involve making you the happiest lass I can." He bent his head toward me and pressed a kiss to my lips, then wrapped his arms around my shoulders as I hugged his waist.

My heart filled with warmth as I returned the kiss. "Ye already have, Dougal. I'm happier than I ever thought I could be, and that's all because of you."

Looking for more sexy werewolves and vampires? Download *Beneath the Broken Moon: Season One*...

AUTHOR'S NOTE

Thank you for reading *The Leopard Who Claimed A Wolf*. I hope you enjoyed it!

It's so amazing to finally share this sixth book in my Cry Wolf series with you! I really enjoyed writing it. Being able to visit Scotland before penning this novel was an amazing experience. It helped shape the whole book, but one scene in particular came about directly because of the trip—the gift shop.

My husband and I were on a sightseeing tour that stopped off at a shop and restaurant that had a sheepdog demonstration. The line for food was super long, and the restaurant ended up running out because of all the tours! Thankfully, we were able to eat, though. :-)

Please consider leaving a review at the retailer's website or on Goodreads, even if it's a line or two. It truly helps!

If you're interested in being the first to know about my next release, sign up for my newsletter.

ACKNOWLEDGMENTS

A very special thank you to my husband for all of your encouragement throughout my writing career, and particularly now as I'm getting back to it all. You're everything I could ask for in a mate.

Julie, my friend and critique partner, I'm grateful for your feedback on the book and, most importantly, your friendship. This writing journey isn't easy, but it's better knowing I'm traveling this road with you.

To my beta readers—Denise and Nicole, you guys rock! I really appreciate your feedback too. It really helped.

Last but not least, my readers. Your support is seriously humbling, and I appreciate you guys so much!

ABOUT THE AUTHOR

New York Times & USA Today Bestselling Author Sarah Mäkelä loves her fiction dark, magical, and passionate. She is a paranormal romance author and a life-long paranormal fan who still sleeps with a night light. In her spare time, she reads sexy books, watches scary movies, and plays computer games with her husband. When she gets the chance, she loves traveling the world too.

- amazon.com/author/sarahmakela
- bookbub.com/authors/sarah-makela
- instagram.com/authorsarahmakela
- facebook.com/authorsarahmakela
- twitter.com/sarahmakela
- goodreads.com/sarahmakela
- pinterest.com/authorsarahmakela

ALSO BY SARAH MÄKELÄ

Currently Available for Free *

Cry Wolf Series

(New Adult Paranormal Romance)

Book 1: The Witch Who Cried Wolf *

Book 2: Cold Moon Rising

Book 3: The Wolf Who Played With Fire

Book 4: Highland Moon Rising

Book 5: The Selkie Who Loved A Wolf

Book 6: The Leopard Who Claimed A Wolf

Cry Wolf Series Boxed Set (Books 1-3)

Beneath the Broken Moon Serial

(New Adult Paranormal Romance)

Part 1 *

Part 2

Part 3

Part 4

Part 5

Season One (Parts 1-5)

Edge of Oblivion

Book 1: The Assassin's Mark

Book 2: The Thief's Gambit

The Amazon Chronicles Series

(New Adult Paranormal Romance)

Book 1: Jungle Heat

Book 2: Jungle Fire

Book 3: Jungle Blaze

Book 4: Jungle Burn

The Amazon Chronicles Collection

Hacked Investigations Series

(Futuristic Paranormal Romance)

Book 1: Techno Crazed

Book 2: Savage Bytes

Book 2.5: Internet Dating for Gnomes *

Book 3: Blacklist Rogue

Book 4: Digital Slave

Courts of Light and Dark

(New Adult Fantasy Romance)

Book 1: Captivated

Book 2: Surrendered

Standalones

Moonlit Feathers

Captive Moonlight

Vera's Christmas Elf

EXCERPT FOR BENEATH THE BROKEN MOON: PART ONE

CARMELA

Bullets peppered the big screen of the *Teatro de la Noche*. Screams rang out around me, and I dropped to the floor, pulling my cousin Chandra down with me. Tension ached in my shoulders, and my heart pounded in my chest like a trapped animal, desperate to escape.

Gunpowder stung my sensitive nose, but through the overpowering scent, I caught a whiff of a hunter heading our way. "Chandra, we have to move."

If Chandra and I didn't get out of here we'd end up dead —or worse, test subjects for the *Cazador*—human hunters ordered to scour the land of nocturnes by the plutocratic government.

"How? They're all around us." Chandra peeked over the seats before dropping back down beside me. "A few of them are chasing down those who ran from the first assault, but two more are heading straight for us." She ran a manicured hand through her honey-brown hair, which was only a shade darker than my own. "Come on. I have a plan. Let's try to sneak out the side door." She crawled in the opposite direction, down the row of seats.

The sight of my cousin's butt cheeks hanging out of her short skirt filled my vision; some things were better left unseen. I lowered my gaze, particularly since Chandra had forgone panties. She almost always held herself with an air of power and purpose. Perhaps that's what it took to get attention from other werewolves. Chandra got it in heaps, but her lower social status stopped a lot of relationships.

While it was a horrible time to second-guess my modest fashion sense, I couldn't help wonder if I should take a lesson from my cousin. My own blouse and dark blue jeans had much less pizzazz. But I doubted my father would allow me to dress like Chandra; we had a privileged image to uphold.

I bit my lip, struggling to turn my thoughts back to the problem at hand. This was all too much. How could we get out of here unscathed when the roar of gunfire continued to close in?

We reached the end of the aisle. Chandra moved to glance over the seat, when a shout came from the opposite end, startling us both.

"Run, Chandra!" I barely kept my voice to a whisper.

She sprinted toward the bright red exit sign at the front of the theater, and I chased after her, trying to keep my pace natural though her long legs made it challenging. Maybe if they suspected we weren't nocturnes, they'd leave us alone.

The stomping of heavy boots on the theater's plush carpets said otherwise. Then again, they weren't opposed to taking their fellow humans down too. The very rich in power thrived on oppressing those less fortunate. What better way to keep the populace down than to have their thugs strike whenever possible.

"We should split up." Chandra shoved a heavy trashcan in front of the door, but that wouldn't be much of an obstacle to the pseudo-military bastards.

"What?" I couldn't believe my ears. "No way. If we do that,

we'll—" The trashcan scraped the cement as the hunters tried to open the door. Maybe she was right. If we were together, there was a better chance of them catching us both. Alone, we might survive the night.

I nodded to her, and we took off in opposite directions down the alleyway behind the *Teatro*. The door slammed open, smacking the wall hard, as I turned the corner and headed toward the main street. I had to find somewhere to hide out before the hunters spotted me again.

In front of me, another group of *Cazador* chased a few werewolves down the main road. I slowed to keep my distance from them, but if I didn't get somewhere fast, they were going to catch me. Ugh. As much as I loved getting out of the house and going to the movies, I wished I'd listened to my instincts tonight and stayed home.

Two sets of feet pounded the sidewalk behind me. Perhaps they'd spotted me before I reached the corner.

I picked up speed a little, pumping my arms as I struggled to keep to a human speed while staying out of range. The temptation to race through the streets nearly drove me to action, but I glanced back, seeing my pursuers for the first time.

One of the men had greying hair and a rounded belly, which explained the slower, heavier footfalls, while the other guy appeared younger and super-athletic. No wonder I was having trouble getting away. If he hadn't been so scary, he might've been attractive. Pure masculine aggression raged through him, tensing his shoulders as his gaze focused solely on me, his prize. Each man carried a large-caliber handgun. I was just glad they were too busy running to try to shoot me...for now, at least.

My sandal hit an uneven patch of concrete in the sidewalk. My body lurched forward, but I caught myself before I could go down. I should've been paying more attention to the street. Up ahead on the opposite side of the road, I spotted a dark alleyway running alongside a row house. If I cut through, I could safely turn up the speed without exposing myself, and lose them.

The older hunter slowed; his breathing had become increasingly labored. He cocked his revolver's hammer, and I darted across the empty road, making a beeline for the alley. The last thing I wanted tonight was to see Dr. Matthews. *Just a little bit farther.* A bullet smacked the ground at my feet, hitting me with fragments of pavement. I bit back a yelp, not wanting to give them the satisfaction of knowing my fear.

"I got this one, old kook," the younger hunter grumbled, and his footsteps slowed too.

Another gunshot pierced the hazy night air. White-hot pain rocked my shoulder, nearly toppling me to the ground. I screamed, unable to hold it in, and picked up speed, no longer caring if I appeared human or not. The faint creak of a door barely registered before a pair of arms wrapped around my waist, jerking me inside the dark row house.

My rescuer softly shut the door, careful not to make a sound, and shoved a hand over my mouth. "Sshhh," he whispered. "I won't hurt you. You're safe." His voice was deep, with an English accent. He pulled me away from the door and hunched down in the darkened room, holding me close, waiting and listening.

Agony clouded my thoughts, but I couldn't let myself lose focus.

Footsteps thundered through the side alley. I stiffened at the sound. The hunters' harsh voices and the clanking of metal were the only differences between them and a herd of cattle. They made no attempt to disguise themselves, taking delight in the fear they provoked. The *Cazador* weren't true predators, but they held power over their fellow humans and the weaker of the nocturnes.

I stayed silent in my mysterious savior's arms. Thoughts of my cousin Chandra sparked inside my mind. She was still out there. What if the *Cazador* found her and killed her as they'd tried to kill me?

This man had saved my life. I needed to do the same for my kin.

His large hand flexed slightly, crushing my mouth. I placed my hand against his wrist, hoping he'd release me, since I no longer heard the disgusting *Cazador* who hunted me like an animal. How had I gotten myself into this mess?

Shifting my weight, I groaned as my shoulder brushed against his smooth chest, my arm hanging limply by my side. The bullet must be impairing my movement. I doubted even shifting into wolf form would fix this right now. What was I supposed to do? Not even my people were immune to blood loss.

The scent of death crept into my nostrils, which could only mean one thing: my savior was a vampire. In this weakened state, he could easily end my life, and I wouldn't be able to stop him.

But why would he save me? Maybe he required his next meal. An icy shiver slithered down the length of my spine. For the first time, I felt real fear.

If only I'd insisted on returning home from the *Teatro* sooner instead of catching the night's second movie, we wouldn't have been there for the raid. Already my energy waned due to the rocky power of the three raging moons. The added exertion of running from the *Cazador* and getting shot strained my body even more.

Somehow, the *Cazador* had known nocturnes frequented the *Teatro*. Who would give that kind of information away? Wolves wanted the same pleasures in life that humans desired.

My savior readjusted his grip on me, brushing against my

upper back. I swallowed a scream, unwilling to alert anyone who might be listening outside this man's home. This *vampire's* home. Clenching my teeth, I pulled at the vampire's wrist. I would not be his victim.

He remained steadfast, proving my weakness. "Don't scream. Don't run. Don't do anything that would force me to hurt you, because I've had a lot of practice." His crisp voice caressed my ear, and his breath moved tendrils of light brown hair, tickling the flesh on my neck. "Do you understand?"

While he meant the words as a threat, I couldn't help the way my body responded to his intensity. I nodded, forcing my thoughts back into place. If he attacked, I needed to remember my Militia training.

The vampire released me, but he stayed still, as if waiting for my next move.

Slowly and carefully, I scooted away and turned to face him. My eyes had gradually adjusted to the darkness, allowing me to see more clearly in the dimly lit room than a human would. What a sight he was. I brushed my fingertips over my sore lips.

Crouching in the shadows, he wore a navy-blue dress shirt with the buttons undone to show off his pale, sculpted chest, and dark jeans that snugly fit his long legs. I'd only seen a few vampires, and none of them had looked this exquisite.

My eyes widened as he ran a hand through his shoulder-length black hair. His gaze had dropped to my lips, and I lowered my hand. Hunger burned in his deep blue eyes; I prayed it wasn't bloodlust.

What was I thinking? Our species didn't see eye to eye on anything except survival. The Feud between vampires and werewolves had raged on for centuries now, since well before bickering humans shot the moon with a nuke after a resource dispute and nearly killed the world's population. Little did my ancestors know just how much and how fast the world would change. Instead of bridging the gap, vamps and wolves had grown even further apart. No one remembered what or whom first started the divide, but neither race spent any effort on diplomatic relations.

Kill or be killed.

I took a deep breath and sat a little straighter. With space between us, my fear lessened. The Militia had taught me to defend myself against hunters and other nocturnes. They made sure I wouldn't be easy prey for the enemy. Of course —they preferred to have my womb protected, since it ensured our race would live on.

Bitterness soured my taste buds, and the urge to spit overwhelmed me.

Admittedly, vampires were the hardest foes to defeat, and I couldn't practice my skills much these days. Not with Father keeping me almost literally a prisoner in my own home.

But if I had to fight this vampire, I would go out having inflicted a lot of pain.

"Why did you help me?" I asked, keeping my gaze on the wall near his head. No way would I look into his eyes. While I was strong, I wasn't stupid. His kind could easily manipulate, and I had no idea what he had in mind.

"I think it was your caramel-brown eyes, love." He leaned into my line of sight, but I looked away. Instead, he closed the space between us in a heartbeat and gently stroked his index finger along my jaw.

The sudden intrusion on my personal space had me jerking away, but with my back so close to the wall, I had nowhere to run. "How could it have been my eyes?" I crossed my good arm under my breasts, but that drew his attention down to my chest. Not what I'd intended. "I'm sure you couldn't have seen them while I was running from the hunters."

With a sensual swipe of his tongue, he licked his lips. His gaze lifted to meet mine, but I quickly averted my eyes. "You caught me."

The cool, sensual touch of his fingers trailed toward my neck, then my shoulder. My breath hitched in my throat as his hand skirted the edge of the wound. Everything in me demanded I move away, but I refused to show weakness.

The vampire sucked in a deep breath, and he let it out in a slow lustful shudder. "You're hurt." He raked his gaze over my body, taking in all of me. "Those eyes must have captivated me again." From what I could see, I doubted my eyes were the only thing he liked.

"Right." His playful answers surprised me; we were supposed to be enemies. If he wanted to drink my blood, he should just say so. But if that were the case, wouldn't he have attacked already? "I should be going. The *Cazador* are long gone by now, so I won't waste any more of your time." I tucked a leg beneath me to climb to my feet, but the vampire grabbed my wrist, holding me still.

Instinct kicked in, and a low growl of warning rumbled from my throat. My teeth sharpened, and the skin on my arms rippled, ready to welcome my beast. But I shut down the change.

He released me and lifted his arms in surrender. "Where are my manners? My name is Derek. I'm afraid I can't let you leave. You're injured, and the hunters could still capture you. Besides, you might tell your wolves where I live." He smiled without flashing any fangs. Others of his kind wouldn't be able to pull that off; he had to be an ancient. "Let me help you. I was once a doctor."

My eyebrows rose in surprise. Such irony. A man who once pledged himself to healing people now drained them of their life's blood. "All I need to do is shapeshift a few times. That'll fix this."

He rose to his feet as if pulled up by strings, then folded his arms. "Shapeshifting isn't going to solve that." Taking in a deep breath, he shook his head. "Not with a wound so severe. If I wanted to hurt you, I would have done so by now. Besides, I just saved you from the *Cazador*."

I hated that he was right. He'd made no move to harm me, and he'd helped when he didn't have to. Sighing, I leaned my head back, wincing as my shoulder touched the wall. "Why did you save me? If the hunters knew, they'd punish you severely."

"More severely than death?" Derek chuckled. "I'd like to see them try."

I stared up at him, a frown tugging at my lips. No one could argue with his logic. He was a vampire; the worst they could do would be to bring him true death. "I'm Carmela. Thanks for the help. Not many would've done that."

"People are afraid of the 'mighty' hunters." He shrugged his broad shoulders, then held out his hand to me. "They're pathetic compared to us."

While I agreed with what he said, I couldn't suppress my wariness at his help. But I didn't have a choice; I was too badly injured to survive the night without treatment. I reluctantly accepted his hand. He lifted me to my feet as if I weighed nothing, then led the way into his living room.

The luxurious room showcased a large velveteen couch with handsome oak inlay in the shape of a creeping rose vine along the back. I leaned down to brush my hand along the forest-green cushion, amazed at the ornate décor, but a trail of my blood slid toward my wrist.

Pulling away, I wrapped my arm around my waist and took in the rest of the room. No way would I ruin his furniture. "This place looks like a museum. It's breathtaking."

"Hardly. It's my home. I have a room upstairs better suited for tending to you." Derek walked toward the banister of the swooping staircase, but he kept his gaze fixed on me as if I'd run at a moment's notice. That should've been closer to the truth. However, I couldn't help my fascination at the way this vampire lived. I'd never seen such nice things before. How many lifetimes had he spent on cultivating his collection? "Coming, Carmela?" He waved for me to follow him.

The sound of my name on his lips pulled me forward. I walked to the steps, but weakness weighed down my limbs. How could I make it home by myself if the thought of climbing the stairs drained me? If he'd been a doctor, I might be okay in his care. Doctors followed a code of ethics. My mother used to be a nurse, and she liked to talk about those days when we were alone.

I took a deep breath, and I only smelled the two of us. Not that I thought I might be walking into a trap, but I couldn't be too careful. My gaze swept back to the living room. I wasn't materialistic, but the blatant show of wealth struck the wishful part of me that hoped for more out of life. I bumped into him as he stopped suddenly on the steps.

"Look, I'm not going to harm you." He cocked an eyebrow at me. "Okay?" Worry tightened his lips for a second, but he flashed a smile.

"Fine. If you say so." The world spun a little, and I clenched the railing in my fist, focusing all of my energy on staying upright. My desire to help Chandra would have to wait. Besides, she'd be okay. She was strong and street-smart. As far as I knew, the *Cazador* had followed me, not her, and I'd be useless searching for her right now.

However, a small part of me whispered that family didn't abandon one another. *Betrayer*, my thoughts hissed, but I shoved them aside.

My legs shook as I reached the top step. Derek watched me carefully but didn't offer his assistance. He probably knew I wouldn't have accepted it. I wouldn't let my weakness get the better of me in front of him, a possible threat. "You'll stay in my spare room. It's a comfortable space to relax while I care for you." I followed him down the hallway, each step harder than the last, and he opened the door for me. "Here you are."

I stayed put and stood up straighter, hoping he'd get the message and go in first, but he didn't. *Right.*

A red paisley bedspread adorned a heavy oak bed with an abundance of matching pillows, befitting royalty. The bedroom was as polished and pristine as the living room. How could I possibly be comfortable with bleeding all over it? If this was how he decked out his spare room, I could only imagine what his room looked like.

I glanced back at the doorway, where he remained. Our eyes met for the first time from across the room, even though I knew the risks. "Where do you want me?" I asked, wincing at how intimate that sounded. "Here?" Dizziness swayed me, and my knees buckled. Strong arms wrapped around me before my body could hit the floor.

Derek's concerned face filled my darkening vision. "Yes, here is fine," he murmured, laying me down on the soft bed. "Don't die on me."